WICKED LOVE

CURSED COVEN

USA TODAY BESTSELLING AUTHOR
LISA MANIFOLD

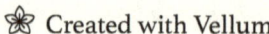

THE MIDNIGHT COVEN

Welcome to the magical world of the Midnight Coven.
Within the pages of our books, you'll find vampires and
demons, witches and fae, dark magic and happily ever
afters. Each Midnight Coven book is a romance novella
featuring characters who occasionally cross over from
book to book, so we hope you'll read them all. You just
never know when your favorite character might show
up again.

Your initiation begins now...

WICKED LOVE

**Has Melasina Cormier met her fiery match in Jasper
Thibodeaux?**

Melasina

I've spent my entire life separating myself from the stain
of my necromancer mother's dishonor. Exiled for using
the dark arts, she had no choice but to break off all
contact and leave the coven. The dreams feel like some
kind of haunted karma where I'm cursed to walk a mile
in my mother's shoes. But when I wake up one morning
covered in mud and smelling like death warmed-over, it
doesn't take long to figure out that the apple didn't fall
far from the necromancy tree.

Enter Jasper Thibodeaux, the magical librarian in
charge of New Orleans, who thinks all the recent grave

robberies are a sign that my mother has returned. He's hot as hell and makes all my senses tingle. In another life, he'd be perfect. Too bad my secret means there's no chance for us; he's the reason my mother's in exile. It doesn't matter how close we get. If he learns I've inherited her necromancy, he won't hesitate to show me the same fate.

When a dark curse threatens everything I've worked so hard to protect, I realize I must face who I am. Do I risk a life of exile or deny my truth for the chance of love?

CHAPTER ONE

Melasina

I rubbed my face, yelping as my hands ground against my eyes. They were gritty, and it hurt. I kept my eyes shut for a moment, not wanting to open them, not wanting to see. I knew, even before I looked, what I was going to find.

Dirt.

Not just dirt, but broken nails, filthy hands, and an odor that could have only come from one place.

A grave.

Inhaling deeply, I could smell the particular scent of what my mom used to call eau de cemetery. Grave dirt was sometimes required for spells, and my mom wasn't afraid to work with it. Not like most of the witches in our coven.

Which had been her downfall.

At the moment, I didn't have time to think about my mom. I needed to focus on my own situation. I opened my eyes to see exactly what I'd expected, although my nails looked worse than anticipated.

The annual ball was tonight, and this was how my nails looked? I might as well put a sign on myself that said 'Grave robber extraordinaire' and be done with it. Turn myself in and get ready to move.

Shit. I needed a manicure. Like, immediately. I'd been waking up like this on and off for the past three weeks, and about half the time, I had dirt under my nails, and a funky smell all over my hands. I added 'manicure' to my mental list of things to get done today.

None of my dithering addressed the problem— mainly, what was I doing at night that I ended up with hands like this in the morning? Also, where was I going? Because I'd woken up with my shoes still on a couple of times. Finally, why couldn't I remember?

All things I had no answer for. I could ask my dad, but after my mom died—well, was exiled and then went away and died—he was pretty much absent, so he had even less idea about me than I did. He certainly wouldn't know about this. Dad was from a family of witches, just as Mom was. But when Mom was exposed for being a necromancer, when she left New Orleans alone because he wouldn't leave, wouldn't do that to himself or me, he closed the door on his witch side.

I wasn't sure he'd done either of us a favor.

He always encouraged me, from a distance, to be

part of the covens, to be a witch. I wondered if it wouldn't have been better for both of us to move away, where no one knew of us. Because there was no way we'd ever be anything other than the Cormiers with a necromancer in the family. At least not for another one hundred years, and even then, it would be passed down as part of the legend of members of our coven. But after fourteen years, this was home. For better or worse.

And I loved my home. I loved the city, even with the floods, and the messes, and all the tourists. I loved the houses, the feel, the music, the architecture—I loved it all. I wasn't going anywhere, despite my occasionally daydreaming about going somewhere where no one knew who I was.

I rolled my eyes at my dithering. None of it solved my problem at this moment. It was merely delaying the inevitable.

As I turned my hands over, I could see scratches on the palms underneath the dirt. Hurrying from bed, I went to the sink in the bathroom and began scrubbing my hands with the nail brush I'd gotten for just this purpose. The soap stung all the little cuts. I ignored it and scrubbed harder. Once my hands were clean, I took the hottest shower known to man.

But the smell wouldn't go away.

There was nothing I could do about this right now. I got myself together and pretended I hadn't woken up with dirty hands again. At some point, I was going to need to figure this out, but I didn't have a clue as to how.

I could ask someone to help me find the memories, but that would mean involving another person in this. If I'd been doing something wrong, I didn't want anyone to know.

I'd learned the lesson of my mother well.

Just as I was ready to head out the door to do my grocery shopping before I got to work, I heard yelling from the laundry room out back. I had a tiny courtyard at the back of my cottage, and the little shed in the corner was connected to the house via a breezeway. I didn't mind the weather, but I hated doing laundry in the rain. You could never tell when it was going to rain in New Orleans. I'd had the breezeway built after I bought the house and got caught toting my clothes inside during a downpour.

"What the hell," I muttered. There shouldn't be anyone in my backyard, much less the laundry room. I raced through the kitchen and breezeway, heart pounding, to find the door to the laundry room unlatched.

Shit. I didn't have my baseball bat, or pepper spray —wait. I *was* a witch. I could justify magic on a non-magic person if they were attacking me. I could also have their memory wiped. OK. I could do this. I took a breath and kicked open the door.

On my black and white lozenge tiled floor, next to my washing machine, lay two bodies. Obviously long dead, and wow, did they smell.

"Oh, my Goddess," I breathed. What in the name of

Hecate were bodies doing in my laundry room? Who had put them there?

A thought struck me. "No," I whispered. "No, it can't be."

"It's about time you came out here," a voice said. "Leaving me out here like this! I deserve better."

I spun around, hands out, protective spells at the ready.

The voice laughed, the ancient cackle of an old, old woman. "That won't help you a bit, *chéri*. I am already quite dead."

"Who are you?" I asked, trying to keep the panic out of my voice.

"I am apparently your latest victim. Come now, you must know. I am the best thing around to help you with those poor wretches on the floor."

This didn't make sense. I looked around and saw a box made of what looked like gold and glass sitting on my dryer. Bones were piled up in the box, and on top of them sat a skull, tilted on its side.

"Very good! You have found me. For the second time," the skull said.

"Who are you?" I whispered.

"You do not know?" There was a silence, and then the skull said, "Very well. If you truly do not know, I am Zelda."

I shook my head.

"Zelda Dupuis." The skull waited again.

Oh, mother of all Goddesses and ancestors. I had

the reliquary box from Magnolia House. The final resting place of the founder of our coven. What the hell was she doing in my house?

As I tried to figure that out, I heard the doorbell ring. "Wait here," I said, whirling around.

"It's not as if I can go anywhere!" Zelda shouted as I ran back through the house. I'd never known that our founder's skull could talk. It never had when we'd been dragged to the house to visit.

I made it to the living room when the doorbell rang again. I slowed to a walk, wanting to calm myself. Taking a deep breath, I opened the door.

The handsomest man I'd ever seen stood on my porch. He had dark hair, and dark, knowing eyes. He was tall, with a commanding presence, but not over-bearing. This was a man at ease with himself. He held out a hand and smiled, and I felt every nerve in my body tingle.

"I'm Jasper Thibodeaux. I'm one of the coven librarians, and I need to speak with you about your mother." His voice was a warm baritone, rich and inviting.

My mouth fell open, but no words came out. Images of this man with far, far less clothing danced through my brain, making me want... oh, Goddess. I needed to stop this, right now. It had been a while since I'd had a boyfriend, but this was ridiculous.

"May I come in?" Jasper asked. His eyes met mine, and I wasn't able to turn away.

Could he come in? Could he stay forever? "Um, yes. Yes, please come in." I stepped back from the door.

"Am I interrupting?"

"I'm just about to go shopping. I mean, to work. I have to shop sometime today, and I have to work," I said. Damn it. I hated that I was fumbling.

"If this is a bad time, I can come back later," Jasper said.

"What? Oh, um, no. No, this is fine."

From the back, Zelda yelled. Damn her! How could she yell so loudly and clearly? When we studied coven history, there was no mention of a mouthy skull residing at Magnolia House. I'd even seen the reliquary, during a tour during middle school. All witches had to learn the local history. Classes were taught at Magnolia House. Even though my dad put up a wall between himself and the community that had sent my mother away, he didn't stop me.

He knew I had a big enough black mark against me as it was.

Back to Zelda—was she just mouthy now that she was here? What was I going to do with her? And me with a coven librarian in my front room. If I'd had a fan, I'd be fanning myself like mad.

Jasper looked up. "You have a roommate?"

"No, a noisy neighbor," I tried to smile and look casual. "What did you want to talk about?"

"May we sit down?" Now it was Jasper's turn to look uncomfortable.

As we both moved to sit down in the living room, I tried to quell the sinking feeling in my stomach. He wanted to talk about my mother. I'd never get away from my mother's legacy.

Never.

CHAPTER TWO

Jasper

*B*ack at the office, this meeting had seemed like it was going to be no big deal.

Just before I'd left last night, I'd gotten a report. There'd been another grave disturbed last night. What was going on? We took grave robbing seriously here in New Orleans, for many reasons. First among them was that those in the magical world who attempted to use the dead were not people of good intentions. No matter the excuse, or the reason—there were never good reasons for dragging the dead out of their rest.

But who could it be? We'd exiled anyone who showed any sign of such activity. I'd seen that happen myself. While there was a great deal of flexibility in our magical world, there were some boundaries that could not be crossed. Attempting to use the dead was one of them. Outside of all the reasons using the dead was wrong, it also risked the chance that we'd be discovered. Part of our success as a coven was our ability to blend in and not attract notice.

The last known necromancer, who was the mother of one our local coven members, was sent away for her poor choices. When I'd read the report after I'd heard about our recent grave robberies, it noted that she had died within a year of her exile. Her daughter and the rest of her family had been model citizens ever since. Probably because they knew that should anything happen, they would be among the first to be questioned.

The Cormier family was one of the oldest families in both New Orleans and in our coven. They'd been here since the founding of our coven. And despite Sariah Cormier and her banishment, they'd been good citizens in our community.

I hated having to investigate, but if I didn't, I'd be derelict in my responsibility. As one of the coven librarians, it was my job to not only keep track of the history and records of our coven, but to make sure that we kept to the rules, to the boundaries. That we kept ourselves discreet. That we didn't draw attention to ourselves.

Grave robbing was not discreet in any way.

Lavinia, my boss, came into my office. We were located in a small estate, by New Orleans standards, near Magnolia House, the coven's headquarters. We'd found that it was better to have coven leadership and records in two different places. Only the librarians and some of the coven leadership knew our exact location, and we had a lot of wards set over the library.

"What's this I hear there has been some disturbance?" she asked, seating herself in a chair in front of my desk.

"Good news travels fast," I said. I'd only had the report for five minutes. "There was an opened grave in St. Louis No. 1." This was the oldest cemetery in the city, and it had some of the best above ground graves. There was an active restoration process ongoing in the cemetery itself, so there was regular activity in the cemetery—but not at night. That's what locking the gates and only allowing guided tours was supposed to help. To keep the vandals and those would cause mischief out.

"How was that managed?" Lavinia asked. "They have that cemetery on lockdown."

"Well, not entirely," I said with a grin.

"Enough," she rolled her eyes. Sometimes our coven needed to go to one of the crypts at night, and the new rules had made things more difficult. But we'd been able to work around it. "Enough that dragging a body out would be noticed."

"Which means," I said.

"That it was done by magic," Lavinia finished.

"My thoughts exactly," I said.

Lavinia shook her head. "I suppose you'd better go and see the Cormiers."

"You don't think they'd actually take the chance, do you?" I asked.

"No," Lavinia got up. "Honestly, I don't. But if you don't go see them, the rumors will start, and that will make it difficult for us to find out who is really doing this. We need to be able to state they had nothing to do with it."

"What?" I asked, laughing a little. "Does that mean you don't believe the absolute worst of that creepy Cormier family?"

"No," Lavinia said. "One person isn't an entire family. But I know exactly how gossip works. You might as well get over there and see the daughter. What's her name?"

"Melasina," I said, checking my notes. "Melasina Cormier."

"Any other children?" Lavina's brows furrowed.

I shook my head. "No, she is an only child. Dad didn't remarry. He's out of the country, by the way. So it's just her."

She sighed. "Well, all right then. Go first thing in the morning." Lavinia breezed out of the room.

That was one of the things I liked best about working for the coven library. There were rules, and boundaries, but there was not a great deal of micromanaging. I'd be free to work this as I chose, as long as I kept Lavinia in the loop.

I looked through my files again. Melasina Cormier was twenty-four, single, lived in the Treme district on Saint Ann, in a small house that had been her family's home. Her father, after his wife had been exiled, took a job with Tulane University in the history department and ended up traveling. Melasina, who was ten at the time, spent a lot of time with a nanny.

Had her mother realized that she would be depriving her child of both parents through her actions? Shaking my head, I gathered up my files. It was after five; I'd go and see Melasina Cormier before I came in to work tomorrow morning.

Because I agreed with my boss. This had nothing to do with the Cormier family. However, checking them off the list would allow us to find the real culprit and deal with them.

Lavinia popped her head back in. "You'll need to let Delphine know. She prefers to be kept in the loop."

Delphine was the current leader of our coven, and she lived in Magnolia House. She'd been the leader for years. While she looked to be in her forties, she was four times that, if not more. I didn't know. I didn't ask her such things. I might get turned into something I wouldn't like.

"You sure you don't want to tell her?" I asked. "Because she's not going to appreciate updates from me, a junior librarian with bad news, when she's in the middle of planning the ball." Our annual ball, which would allow for a blessing for all those present, was tomorrow night.

"I hadn't thought of that. Never mind, then. I'll talk to her when I go over tonight. Let me know as soon as you talk with the Cormier girl. That'll give me something to tell her."

"I'm going to see her tomorrow morning before work. I'll call you on my way in," I promised. I'd taken my laptop home, going over the files once more so that I didn't show up on Melasina Cormier's doorstep without all the facts.

Which is why not only had I come here with questions about the grave disturbances, but a few more things. There had been a number of people adding to the file of Sariah Cormier, and not only was it interesting, but the information within was extremely contradictory. When I'd looked at the main investigator of the case, it was Talia Dumond, the former Head Librarian who had trained me. Talia had since retired, but she was second to none.

Or so I thought until I saw the handwritten notation on one of the last pieces of paper in the file. I had to read it again, and then I followed up with the online records—we still had too much paper, but it was hard to convince our older members that paper wasn't the best thing.

This couldn't be. I shook my head, and went to bed, the lines I'd read seared into my brain. I couldn't shake them. When had I seen this file before? There was a hint of memory, but it was just out of reach.

And so, armed with all the questions that had come up for me, that was how I found myself sitting across from the most gorgeous woman I'd ever seen. She was tall, but not as tall as my 6'2 frame. She had long hair that was dark as the moonlit sky and wavy, falling down around her face and shoulders. Her skin had a creamy cast, and she had light green eyes. It was a striking look with her hair, and I couldn't look away. A surge of lust came over me. I wanted to run my hands through her hair, pull her to me, bend her head back, exposing that creamy neck and—

The neighbor she'd mentioned yelled from the backyard again.

"Your neighbor is up early," I said, smiling, trying to regain my bearings and calm myself.

Melasina whipped her head around so quickly I wondered if she'd hurt herself.

"Yes, she's a pain sometimes," she said. Her voice was tight as she gave me a thin smile.

Something was off here.

"Well, let's get to this, and I'll get out of your hair," I said. Pulling out my laptop, I opened it. I also pulled out the file, setting it on the small table in front of me.

"What is this about?" Melasina asked. She looked nervous.

"This is rather awkward, so I'm just going to put it

out there. There's been some activity in the graveyards around here."

Her eyebrows went up, and the anxious expression disappeared as though it had never been there. "So you thought you'd come and visit the nearest member of the Cormier family?" Her voice was harder, and there was none of the nervousness I'd thought I'd heard only a moment before. "The only member left in New Orleans?" She asked, sarcasm dripping from her words.

"It's just a matter of covering our bases," I said.

Melasina leaned forward. She was angry. "My mother was one person. She wasn't our entire family. And after you lot kicked her out, she died! So thanks for that! But regardless of what she did, that has nothing to do with me! I've been a model citizen!"

"Um, well, yes." I'd expected some pushback, but this was over the top. " So you have no idea about who might have disturbed any local graves?"

"None," Melasina said.

"And a few questions about your mother. Did you attend her funeral?"

"What?" She was taken aback at my question.

"Did you attend her funeral?"

Melasina looked down. "No. My dad went, but he didn't feel I needed to go. He took me to her grave about a year after that, but I wasn't there for the service."

I nodded, making a note in the open file. That made sense with what I'd found. The funeral had been small, hasty, and secretive.

"Why do you ask?" Melasina was looking at me intently.

"Oh, I was checking some of the things in my notes," I said, not wanting to give any of my suspicions away.

"I'm sure you have extensive notes. Talia Dumond was very thorough in her prosecution of my mother," her face twisted.

"Um, yes," I said. Talia was my mentor, the one who brought me into the library, who showed me the way to work within our coven, the library, the rules, everything. She'd been the one who helped me make the transition to an active member in our coven. She was like a mother to me. Which made this all the more difficult.

"Was there anything else?" Melasina stood up.

I finished typing my notes, and then closed the laptop as I got up. "Do you have any idea if there was someone who worked with your mother before she left? Any ideas, any at all?"

Her face closed as her eyes narrowed, which gave me a pang. That made no sense—I'd just met her. Why did I care that she didn't like me? "No, Jasper, I don't. I don't know why you'd think I would. Like I couldn't learn from what happened to my mother? Like I'd risk my life?" She shook her head. "You people at the library are supposed to know history. Maybe learn some. I'm just a plain old witch, not a trained librarian, and even I know that necromancy isn't the way to go." Melasina stood and walked to the door and opened it.

I admired her long legs and graceful form. Lust nearly overtook me again.

But Melasina's intention was clear. She was done with the discussion. Normally, I didn't find myself at a loss for words, but right now, I didn't know what to say. I had no more reason to hang around.

"Thank you for your time," I said. I stood up. I had more that I wanted to say, that I wanted to talk about, but what was it? My head felt muddled, my thoughts scattered.

"Of course. I'm law and order all the way," Melasina said sarcastically.

The door shut behind me with a click, and I found myself on her porch. Wishing that I was still inside. "What just happened?" I asked myself, turning around to see her front door. "I wasn't done." I looked at the closed door. "I wasn't done."

Despite my words, my feet moved down of the little porch, taking me toward my car.

CHAPTER THREE

Melasina

I should be frightened. The coven leadership —well, let's be honest. The coven law enforcement, which was what the librarians were—had already noticed the graves. And here I was with two bodies and a mouthy skull in my back shed.

Shit.

How had this happened? I waited to make sure that Jasper Thibodeaux—who, by the way, was the hottest guy I'd seen in ages, damn it—got into his car. He walked slowly, the effects of my spell, no doubt. As soon as he'd mentioned my mom, I told him what I knew, and cast a 'get the hell out' spell on him. It had all but moved him out the door. Finally, he started the car and drove away. Thank Goddess. Once I saw his car turn the corner, away from me, I sped back to the laundry shed.

"How did you get here?" I asked Zelda the skull.

"You brought me. How else would I get here?"

"Oh sweet Goddess. How did I manage that? You're normally in the crypt at Magnolia House!" The thought scared the living daylights out of me. If anyone discovered this, I'd be out of New Orleans, and my coven, and the entire world of witches so fast I wouldn't know what hit me. I'd never live freely again.

"You know, it would lovely if you'd fix me," Zelda remarked.

"Fix you how?" I was struggling with the fact that I was chatting away with a box of bones.

"I'm tilted and it makes it hard to see what's going on," Zelda said. "Just reach in and set my head upright."

"You can see?"

"Well, not with my skull, no," Zelda said as though I were a slow child. "But my spirit has been kept with my bones. So you may address my skull as though I were there before you."

"I may address you? Well thank you," I said, unable to hide the sarcasm in my voice.

"Don't take a tone with me, young lady!" Zelda squawked. "Nice shellwork with that young man, by the by."

"I'm not taking a tone, and thanks for the compliment," I sighed, tired already. It wasn't even nine in the morning, and I felt like I'd already run a marathon.

"How in the hell am I going to get these bodies out of here?"

"Same way they came in."

"I have no idea how they came in," I snapped. "I don't remember bringing you here, and I can't imagine that you were quiet."

Zelda didn't respond immediately. Then the she said, "No, I was actually watching to see what was happening. I could tell you were not entirely yourself, and I couldn't see that you meant me any harm, so I waited, and watched."

"And what do you think now?" I asked, almost afraid to hear the answer.

"I think you have a problem, *chéri*. You are not awake when you do these things." There was a note of warning in Zelda's voice.

"Yeah, this is what got my mom into trouble," I said, running a hand through my hair. "I can't put them back today."

"No, that wouldn't be prudent," Zelda said. "But use magic to send them home."

"I don't know where I got them!" I threw up my hands in disgust. Jasper Hottie Thibodeaux hadn't said which cemetery or cemeteries were disturbed.

"I can help you with that," Zelda said.

"It all needs to wait," I said. "I need to go shopping. I need a manicure," I rubbed at my scratched hands. "I need to get to work." I worked as a website designer, and while I worked at home, I had to meet deadlines and clients online throughout the day. At least I'd be able to be around and make sure no one discovered my crazy and completely illegal additions to the back shed. "How in the hell did this happen?" I muttered. I made to leave the shed. I needed to go to the grocery store, too, but it looked like food was down on the important list.

"You can't just leave me here," Zelda said.

"What am I supposed to do with you?"

"Bring me with you. I've been stuck in the crypt for years. I'd like some company."

I stared at the box. This felt surreal, insane almost. After everything that happened with my mom, I didn't step one toe outside the lines. No experimental magic, no creating spells. Nothing but standard, normal, acceptable spell craft.

And still, I ended up with a talking skull in my shed.

"Oh, all right. But if anyone knocks, I'm putting a drape over your box."

Zelda didn't reply immediately. Then she sighed— how did a spirit do that? "Very well. I accept your offer."

"Well, I'm so glad," I said.

Zelda apparently missed the sarcasm. "As am I. I know this was not your choice, *chéri*, but I am glad for the company. And it's exciting to have a mystery to solve!"

"I don't exactly think of my life as a mystery," I said, carefully balancing the reliquary as I left the shed. I locked the door. I didn't need anyone snooping around in there. Not until I could get my grisly visitors back where they belonged.

"But it is a mystery!" Zelda crowed. "Why are you moving when you are not awake? Have you always walked in your sleep?"

I shook my head as I sat the box carefully on the side table in my tiny office. "No, never. I've only been waking up with dirty hands for—" I stopped.

"Yes?" Zelda prompted.

"The last three weeks."

"But you didn't bring home any corpses before now?" The laughter had faded from her voice.

"I haven't done laundry in four days and there were no bodies in there when I did my laundry," I said, my own voice shaky. I sat down in my office chair, feeling a hundred years old and completely defeated. "I'm so screwed."

"You don't have to be," Zelda remarked.

"Shouldn't you be turning me in to the coven police?"

Zelda made a noise. "Perhaps. But I do not sense harm from you. There is an air of danger about you, although I don't sense it coming from you personally. It's more all around you, *chéri.*"

"That makes me feel so much better."

"It should. Now enough sulking. We have work to do."

"What do you mean?" I asked. How was it I was being bossed around by a skull in a box?

"We need to discover what it is that has set you off. Why are you heading out into the night now? What are you seeking? Is this your will, or another's?"

Her words sent a chill through me. "That's all well and good, but I need to go out. Then I need to work."

"Well, go if you must. But you and I must work today. Otherwise, who knows what happens tonight?"

"You really don't understand the idea of softening the blow, do you?" I asked.

Zelda laughed. "Of course I do, but where is the sense in that? You have a problem, and I am a fresh set of eyes for your problem."

"You're not a fresh set of anything," I muttered.

"I heard that, and while technically that is true, what is also true is that I have been part of assisting the coven leadership for many years."

"Even now?" I asked. Sweet Goddess, if they talked to her regularly, they would know she was missing, and then getting her back to the crypt would be nearly impossible.

There was a moment's silence, and then Zelda spoke, sounding stiff. "No, as of late, the coven leadership has needed less of my time."

Oh. I knew hurt pride when I heard it. But for me, that was great. "That means it will be easier to get you back where you belong," I said.

"How do you plan to do that?" Zelda asked.

"I have no idea. I don't even know how to get the bodies back to their graves," I said.

"I can help you," she said eagerly. "There are spells that will return them."

"Are you sure? You've been gone a long time," I said.

"Are you questioning my ability?" Zelda asked. "The founder of your coven?"

"No, I'm not. I'm nervous," I said.

"Understandable," Zelda replied. Her voice had changed to that of a teacher.

I wasn't sure if that was a good or a bad thing. "Listen, I need to get things done today, somehow get those bodies back, and get myself together for the coven ball tonight."

"You can't miss that," Zelda agreed.

"Not when there is some question about me," I said. "I swear, I'm never going to get past that."

"Well, let's get started. What are you wearing tonight?"

"I don't know," I said.

"That's your first task then," Zelda said.

I spent the rest of the day dealing with work tasks. I left the grocery shopping. I'd have to deal with it tomorrow. I kept a hunk of cheese in the back of the fridge. After lunch of cheese and some slightly old cucumbers, I went and got a manicure, asking the tech to please pamper my hands. I needed to look innocent as hell tonight.

Just after dark, I stood in front of the mirror in my room, turning from side to side. Zelda sat on the dresser on my left.

"You look wonderful, although you're showing an awful lot of skin," she said.

"Maybe to you," I said. "I'm pretty modest." My long dress was fitted, with a mermaid flair at the bottom. It was midnight blue, and the fabric sparkled as I turned from side to side.

"There's no room for me," Zelda said.

"What?" I spun around to look at her.

"Well, you need to take me with you. What if you're bespelled by someone? You won't be able to see that. I will."

"You have got to be kidding," I said.

Zelda didn't reply.

"No," I said.

She didn't say anything. The silence said it all.

"I don't have a bag big enough for that," I said. "And what if I'm caught with you?"

"You won't be. We can set a concealment spell over me," she said.

"How convenient," I muttered.

"Yes, it is," Zelda said cheerfully. "That's the beauty of having an elder on your side."

"That's what we're calling it? Having an elder on my side?" I asked.

"If you're wise," her tone held a warning.

I stifled a laugh. After I finished my makeup, and looked my hair over once more, I went to my closet to see what bag to carry. I'd planned on a small evening bag, but that wasn't going to work with a skull that needed to fit in there. I found a black bag and made sure Zelda fit.

"This is quite cramped," her voice came from my bag.

"Listen, you need to deal," I said. "And you can't just shout at me from my bag. It'll look really weird."

"What's the point of me going then?" Zelda was exasperated.

"You can stay home," I suggested.

"No, missy, I cannot. Very well. I shall be quiet. But I'm watching."

I laughed then, not bothering to hide it. "I'll remember that. There's not going to be much to see."

"We'll see about that," Zelda snapped.

Together with Zelda, I cast a concealment spell. No one could see her in my bag, even if the bag fell and she rolled out. The thought of being caught with her made me sweat just thinking about it.

"Let's go," I said. I'd called for a Lyft, because parking around Magnolia House was shit. The driver was a tall woman who thankfully wasn't very talkative. I didn't have the energy for anything extra.

Walking in, I could see how the coven had gone all out for this. They usually did, but I hadn't been to the annual ball the last couple of years. I just didn't see the point, and I was tired of always being the object of whispered conversations. I doubted it would be any different tonight, but with the librarian guy—who was still super hot, and whom I found myself thinking about more than once today—showing up at my house, I didn't have a choice.

"Melasina!" Delphine, the leader of our coven came over and air-kissed me on both cheeks. "It's so nice to see you." She stood back, surveying me. "You look... different." Her brow furrowed. "What have you done with yourself?"

I shrugged, feeling my neck get warm. "I'm here? I haven't been to the ball the last two years."

She stared at me a moment longer. "Perhaps. There is something about you," her eyes moved over me slowly, "that feels different."

Oh, shit. Could she see Zelda? Feel her? Oh, Goddess.

Then her brow cleared, and Delphine smiled. "Well, it's good to see you. Don't be such a stranger," she said. She patted my hand and moved away.

Was there a warning in her words?

I walked through the entryway, moving to the ballroom. There were people I knew—I wondered if my dad would be here. How sad it was that I didn't know. How sad that we didn't talk. I straightened my shoulders, shrugged off the whispers, hitched up my bag that had Zelda's skull in it, and headed into the fray.

The first person I saw, before I even had the chance to get a drink, was Jasper Thibodeaux.

Damn it.

His eyes met mine, and a smile turned up the corners of his wide, delicious mouth. He actually looked happy to see me. Sadly, I thought he might be the only person who was. Jasper came toward me, still smiling.

My insides clenched, and I felt every nerve ending in my body wake up as he touched my arm.

"Hi, Melasina. I was hoping I'd see you tonight."

CHAPTER FOUR

Jasper

*M*elasina looked startled when I touched her arm. Her cheeks turned pink. Well, at least I thought they did. It could have been the lighting.

"Oh, um... hi. Hello. Nice to see you again." She looked down for a moment, seeming flustered.

I hoped it was because of me, but that was probably hoping for too much. It also could have been because she cast a spell on me this morning, essentially kicking me out of her house, too. The fact that it had worked so well meant one of two things: either she was very, very strong, or I was completely taken with her, and stupid. I could have written a report that ripped her for the spell, but I decided I wanted to see what would happen if I pretended I hadn't noticed.

Back to her strength or my foolishness: It could be both. I wasn't sure which one I wanted it to be. Regardless, the question remained as to why she'd booted me out? "I was hoping to talk with you some more," I said with a smile designed to put her at ease.

Melasina looked up as she clutched the bag on her shoulder closer to her. "Why?"

"Well, when I came to see you, I didn't get a chance to talk about everything I wanted to." Apparently, my charm wasn't working here. Even with me pretending I hadn't noticed her spell. I should be mad, but I was intrigued.

Her eyes narrowed. "What, tossing around more accusations? If you want to talk more, let's do it at the library, on the record." She pushed past me, obviously done with the conversation.

I caught up with her, trailing right behind her as she took a glass of champagne from a passing waiter. "No," I say quietly in her ear. "It's about your mother."

Melasina stops, whirling around to face me. "What about my mother? Haven't we covered it all? Isn't it enough that she's gone?"

"Well, I've had some disturbing reports," I began.

Melasina cut me off. "You people! You're all the same! My family is trashed, and there's no coming back from that. My dad and I are suitably cowed, and we don't want any trouble. Can we just leave it at that?" Her voice ended on a note that told me this was still some-thing that brought her grief.

I felt like a jerk, which didn't normally happen. Protecting the coven, making sure that we were safe, weren't discovered—that was my job. My responsibility. But I felt bad for forcing this conversation on Melasina Cormier. Was I going soft?

No. She'd kicked me out of her house. There was a reason for that. And I was going to figure out what it was.

"What is that?" Melasina wondered. "Whoa. Holy hell, what is she doing here?" She was looking over my shoulder.

I turned, and I'm pretty sure my mouth fell open.

Melasina moved next to me, her shoulder brushing up against me. Normally, I'd be thrilled, and my cock was, but the scene unfolding outside the open doors in the garden held my attention.

A beautiful, dark-haired woman had appeared in the middle of the garden where Delphine, the coven leader, planned to be later to deliver the blessing. The witches in the garden had noticed her and the murmuring of the crowd grew.

"Wasn't she banished?" Melasina asked me out of the side of her mouth. "Did she really do it? Or was she just off the popular girls' list?"

Her skepticism, given what had happened to her mom, was understandable. I looked around to see where any of the leaders were, and none were nearby. Shit. "She really did it. She used some very dark magic."

Thea, our most recently banished witch, stood in the center of the garden. Her dark hair moved around her, possibly as a result of the magic she was getting ready to cast. She threw up her hands and began to speak.

"How the hell did she get in here?" I asked, not really expecting an answer. "The wards should have kept her out." Magnolia House was well warded, which meant someone like Thea—no longer coven, and banished—should have never been able to get in here.

Thea looked around, a tiny smile tilting up one side of her lips.

"'Neath silver moon or dark of night
In shadow deep or brightest light
From this hex none shall be spared
For wrath knows not peace nor care
Betrayers! Gather close and hear
I damn you to your darkest fear
I bind you to dread's cold embrace
Until your truth you boldly face"

Her arms up, she stopped, and then the force of the spell hit the garden.

It was as though a bomb had gone off. The witches closest to where she stood fell. The flowers and plants near Thea flattened. As the shock hit me, I fell backward.

A moment later, Melasina fell on top of me.

I blinked. The words of the spell rang in my ears, and my cock, which had been distracted at her touch, woke to the fact that a gorgeous woman was lying on top of me. Worse, said woman was moving. Wiggling. This was not the time to be thinking about her on my cock. In any fashion.

Melasina rolled off me and I scrambled to my feet, holding out a hand for her as I looked into the garden. Thea was gone, and there were witches lying on the ground. Some were bleeding from their noses, and I saw one man rubbing blood off his ear.

"Are you all right?" I leaned down to ask Melasina.

"What the hell was that?" she asked.

"I think we were all just cursed," I said. I didn't know for sure, but it felt like it. I needed to get a pen and paper, write down what I'd heard. "Stay here." I squeezed her hand, and hurried to where Thea had been.

There was nothing left but a scorch mark on the garden stones.

"What was that?" I felt a hand on my shoulder and turned around to see my boss, Lavinia.

"A grade A, no fucking around curse, if I had to take a guess," I said.

"How did she get in here?"

"I wondered that myself."

"It's all hands on deck, Jasper. We'll need to go over this entire place with a fine-toothed comb."

I sighed. I thought I'd had other plans, but... I turned to see where I'd left Melasina standing at the door to the garden.

She was gone.

Why in the world would she leave? Especially now, with what had just happened? My sense of unease grew.

"Come on," Lavinia said. "We might as well get started." She patted my shoulder and walked back to the house.

"I'll be there in a moment," I said. I walked back to the ballroom and looked around. Melasina wasn't anywhere in the room. She'd left.

Why? As I continued to look around, I saw a glint on the floor. It was a necklace. I reached down, and as I picked it up, I realized it was Melasina's. A small diamond pendant on a delicate gold chain. I'd noticed it when I was ogling her earlier.

Despite the mess of this moment, and the fact that Melasina was gone, I grinned. I had a perfect excuse to see her again. Even though I'd been unable to talk to her about her mother again, even though she'd cast me out of her house with magic—now I had a reason to seek her out. I wanted to know what the reports I'd been given meant. I wanted to know why she'd sent me away. I also wanted to see Melasina again. I was honest that being around her was part of it.

Just not yet. Whatever Thea had done had to take precedence. Even as I found I didn't care why Thea was here, or what she'd done. I was much more interested in Melasina Cormier.

For lots of reasons.

~

*A*fter an hour, we were able to determine that one, Thea was long gone, two, she'd laid a curse on the house, but no one was sure exactly how to break it, and finally, that we had no idea how the curse was going to affect those who'd been in Magnolia House. Nothing seemed to be off, outside of being knocked on my ass, but I'd heard the curse. It had been powerful. And words like that, said that way, were extremely powerful. To me, they spoke of fear. And fear was one of the most powerful things in the world.

I could still hear Thea, her words echoing through the garden, feeling them in my bones. I'd written down what I remembered, and it would be compared with everyone else. Not to mention, someone would access their memories. We'd have the exact wording by tomorrow.

Lavinia, who'd been leading some of the librarians through the events in the garden once more, looked over at me. "You have it all written down and turned in?"

I nodded. "Yes. It's done."

She sighed and spoke in a voice meant only for me. "Well, I don't think we're all going to die, although I'm not going to say that with any surety. Why don't you go home? I'll see you tomorrow. This is going to mean late hours for a while. Damn that Thea."

A shout from inside the house grabbed everyone's attention. Delphine came out toward where we stood. As she stopped in front of us, I could see that her mouth was pinched, and she was angry.

But Delphine was a good leader, and she didn't explode, or make a scene.

"What is going on?" Lavinia asked.

"The crypt has been broken into," Delphine said quietly, the worry coming through her words.

"Was anything taken?" I asked.

"I'll need records of the inventory of anything stored there," Delphine said. "At the moment, there's only one thing that I can say is missing for sure."

"Which is?" Lavinia asked.

"The reliquary," Delphine whispered.

"Oh, shit," I exclaimed before I remembered where I was.

Delphine glanced at me and nodded. "Exactly. That's why Thea was able to get in here. With the reliquary gone, the wards around the house were broken."

"Then let us help set the wards again," Lavinia said briskly. "They won't be as strong without the Founder's reliquary, but they'll keep Thea out."

"I think she's done her damage," I said.

That earned me side eye from both my boss and my coven leader. I shut up, and followed them into the house to help reset the wards. Once we'd finished, Lavinia sent me home.

But I wasn't headed home. I felt the necklace in my pocket. I was going to return this to Melasina, and... and what?

Try and finish the conversation that I'd started. It wasn't that late. I found it odd that she'd left. As I pulled up in front of her cottage, I could see the lights on in the front room.

Good.

I knocked on the door, and I could hear her moving around. After a moment, the door was yanked open.

"Oh, it's you," Melasina said. Her tone indicated she wasn't overjoyed to see me.

Which gave me a pang, but I brushed it aside.

"Yes, I wanted to return this to you," I held out the small gold necklace.

One hand went to her neck, and Melasina's expression relaxed. "I didn't even realize it had fallen off. Thank you," she reached for it.

"May I come in?" I asked.

Her hand stopped midair, and she looked at me for what seemed like a long moment. Then she sighed. "All right." She took the necklace from me and turned from the door.

I followed her in.

Melasina went to a small chair next to the fireplace. "What do you want, Jasper?" She sounded tired.

"I keep trying to talk with you about your mother, and we keep being interrupted," I smiled. I was inordinately pleased she'd let me come in, that I got to be around her again. "And you rushed me out of here this morning," I added, wanting to see her reaction.

She flushed.

I was right. She'd used magic. Which should worry me, but I pushed that aside as well.

"I've told you everything about my mother. And what the hell happened tonight?"

"Why'd you leave?" I asked.

"There was nothing for me there. I'm not exactly welcome, and frankly," Melasina ran a hand through her hair, "People tend to look at me and see things that aren't there, particularly when something negative happens. I just left before anyone looked at me and started making assumptions."

I nodded. It made sense, and honestly, it made me feel ashamed. I'd written her off before, just as everyone else had. Before I'd met her. Even with the whole toss me out of her house using magic thing.

"What did you want to talk to me about?"

"If you recall," I leaned back, "I asked you if you'd gone to your mother's funeral, and for anything you remembered during that time."

She nodded.

"The reason I ask is that we've had a report of someone seeing Sariah," I said, watching her carefully.

Melasina blinked, and her mouth fell open, just a little.

It was adorable, and I wanted to kiss her, make her mouth fall open even more as she said my name, first softly, and then louder, as she screamed... I shook my head. I had to get control over my thoughts.

"How can that be?" she asked.

"I don't know," I said, shrugging. "Which is why I wanted to speak with you. Not only because of the disturbed graves, but because of what I'd read in the report."

Her face and neck flushed again. "You have a report on me?" She was angry.

"Yes, Melasina, we do. We keep records of everything. Although it wasn't a report on you but your mother. A note had been added recently that reported seeing someone who resembled your mother. Had you not hurried me out of here, I would have told you about it this morning."

Her eyes met mine and skittered away.

Busted.

"Why'd you push me out with magic? You know that's not—"

"Yes, I know it's not allowed!" Melasina burst out. "I'm well aware of everything that's not allowed!"

"And yet you did it anyway," I stood up, moving closer to her.

"Because I didn't want to talk about my mother yet again!" Melasina stood up as well, her hands clenched at her sides, her eyes sparking with fire.

I took another step toward her, closing the distance between us.

"Just please go away, Jasper," Melasina said. "If my mother is not dead, there's nothing I know about it. I can't help you," she put her hands out to push past me.

I caught her arm. "Are you sure about that?" I asked. "After all, we both know you use magic when it's not completely appropriate."

She stared at me, her anger spilling off her like water coming over the levees. Then with her free hand, she reached up and grabbed my head, pulling me down close to her.

I was so surprised I didn't say anything.

Her lips crashed into mine, and whatever else was on my mind was lost.

CHAPTER FIVE

Melasina

I hadn't meant to kiss him, but even as angry as I was, he was so hot, so tempting, that I just acted without any thought.

As his lips met mine, I felt my body go up in flames. He felt amazing. It felt so, so good to be touched. To touch someone else.

Jasper groaned, and he let go of my arm to wrap both his arms around me, one hand tangling in my hair. He devoured my lips, nipping at them as he kissed me. The scrape of his teeth against my skin made me wet.

My arms snaked around his neck, pulling him closer to me. His lips moved down my neck, and my head fell back. I moaned. He felt so good.

Jasper slid his hands under my tee shirt, up my back. One hand came around and lifted up my tee shirt to expose my breasts. I felt my nipples pebble under the breeze from the ceiling fan, and Jasper bent his head to take one in his mouth.

I felt a rush of wetness between my legs as he suckled on the nipple, his other arm cradling me, supporting me.

Then he moved his mouth to the other nipple, and the feel of his teeth made me gasp. "Oh, Goddess."

Jasper stilled. He stood, letting my tee shirt fall. "I—I didn't mean—" he began.

"I did," I said, feeling bolder than I'd felt in ages. "Don't stop."

"Melasina—"

I pulled him toward me, moving us to my room. There were two small rooms on the side of my house. The one in the front of the house was my office. I'd made the second room my bedroom.

At the doorway, he balked. "No, we can't."

I stopped. "We don't have to," I said, feeling bereft at his rejection. I straightened my tee shirt. "I'm sorry. I had the wrong idea." I took a step to move around him.

"No, you didn't," Jasper's voice was raspy and low. For the second time that night, his arm stopped me. Slowly, gently, he pulled me to him, and walked into my room with me. He turned, and sat on the edge of my bed. "You didn't have the wrong idea at all." He paused again. "Are you sure?" he asked.

"Are you?" I cupped his face in my hands. It didn't matter that he was a librarian, that I was hiding secrets —none of that mattered. What mattered was right now, the two of us, together. This was right. I didn't know how I knew, but I knew.

"Yes," Jasper said. He lifted my shirt, and this time, he drew it over my head.

I reached down and slid his jacket off. I'd gotten home and changed into shorts and a tee shirt, but Jasper was still in his suit from the ball. Once his jacket was on the floor, I undid his tie, and then unbuttoned his shirt.

All the while he watched me with dark eyes that held hunger and desire. Staring into his eyes and seeing his desire made me feel strong and powerful.

He reached for my shorts, and tucking his thumbs in the waistband, slid them down, taking my panties with the shorts. I stepped out of them, and stood before him, naked.

His eyes were hooded as he gazed at me. "You are beautiful," he said, his voice husky.

I stepped closer to him, and he wrapped his arms around me again, his head at my stomach. He was still for a moment, and then I felt his lips against my skin. He kissed my stomach, and then his mouth followed his hands to my hips.

It had been a long time since I'd let anyone see me naked, much less this guy. But he felt so good, and his hands on me felt right.

"I'm sure," Jasper murmured into my hipbone. "I want you."

I reached down and tilted his head up. "Good," I said.

He stood up, turning me around, and sat me down on the bed.

"Lie back," Jasper grinned as he spoke.

I couldn't help but to grin back, and I let myself relax onto the bed. I made to scoot up, but he grabbed my legs.

"No," was all he said.

With my legs hanging over the edge of the bed, Jasper knelt down between them. He shuffled around, and I heard him kick something.

Oh, shit. My bag.

"Hey!" Zelda hissed.

"Oh," I sighed loudly, pushing myself up onto my elbows.

Jasper's eyes met mine, questioning.

"I want to watch you," I said, making my voice husky. The thought of watching him do what I thought he was about to was making me wet, but I didn't need him to turn around and see my bag. Zelda's skull was still in the bag. I hadn't had a chance to take her out before Jasper knocked on my door.

Thankfully, he didn't turn around, but bent down and kissed between my legs, making my head fall back.

Watch. I needed to watch. At least for a little bit. I forced my head back up.

Jasper's eyes were on me as his tongue dipped into me, and watching him watch me was so sexy, I could have come right there in that moment.

My legs jerked and his hands came up to hold them still. He leaned into me more, pushing his tongue further inside of me, and then out, in and out, and then licking around my folds.

Then he circled my clit, slowly, deliberately.

I nearly came off the bed.

With slow, careful movements, he licked, and sucked, and nearly drove me to distraction. Every time he brought me closer, my legs would tense, and Jasper would stop me from moving too much.

It made everything even hotter.

I wanted to come, and he'd brought me close a few times, stopping just before I arched up in release.

Bastard. He knew what he was doing. I could tell from the glint in his eyes.

His tongue got faster, moving in tighter circles around my clit, and then he took my clit in his mouth and sucked on it.

"Oh, Goddess!" I said in a whisper.

Jasper sucked harder, and I felt myself falling over the edge, my legs coming up and my back arching. He kept sucking and I came hard. Jasper didn't stop, and I came again, crying out in a voice I didn't recognize as my own.

He gently moved away from me, and my legs relaxed.

As I watched, he bent his head to the side and took off his shoes and socks. Then he stood, and undid his pants. When they dropped to the floor, his cock sprang free, and I smiled in appreciation. It jutted out before him. I couldn't wait to get up close and personal.

"I need you," Jasper growled.

I pushed myself onto the bed, moving up towards the head. Leaning over, I pulled open the drawer on the bedside table, scrabbling inside. Finally, I came out with a small foil packet.

Wordlessly, Jasper took it from me, and rolled it on, never taking his eyes from me.

I found his intent stare to be both intoxicating and disconcerting. I couldn't remember the last time someone had watched me with such intensity. With such desire. Because they wanted to. I wanted him to take me, make me his—and the thought shook me as much as everything he was doing.

He crawled onto the bed and settled between my legs. His cock nudged at the entrance to my pussy, and I found I didn't want to wait. I spread my legs, and thrust my hips up at him, taking him in.

Jasper drew in his breath, stopping as he entered me. Then he thrust forward, seating himself to the hilt.

I felt stretched, filled. My hands went to his shoulders and then down his back to his ass, pulling him to me.

Jasper reached with one hand behind him, and pulled my hand away. He moved it up over my head.

Then he took the other, bringing my hands together. He covered my hands in his, and thrust.

"Oh!" I cried out.

CHAPTER SIX

Jasper

*W*atching her come—twice—as I buried my face in her nearly made me lose control. It was the most gorgeous, sexy thing I'd ever seen. And through it all, Melasina watched me, her eyes never leaving mine.

I couldn't look away. Everything about her, her smell, her taste, the feel of her—it made me want to possess her, take her for mine. I'd never felt this way before. As I moved her hands up over her head, and then held them there as I thrust into her, I thought, I could die right now and be happy.

She spread her legs wider, and I pulled back, and

squeezed her hands as I thrust forward into her again. I could feel her wetness as she clenched around me. It was the most amazing thing I'd ever felt.

No one had ever felt the way that Melasina did right now, with my cock buried in her. No one had ever made me feel the way I did with my face between her legs, watching her lose herself because of me.

In and out, in and out, I thrust hard and deep each time, wanting all of her. She didn't look away, her mouth falling open.

"Next time, my cock goes in that mouth," I murmured.

An answering wetness in her pussy told me that she liked that, a promise of what was to come.

I felt myself getting closer, and I thrust harder, and faster, unable to keep the slow tempo I'd started with. I wanted all of her, and I couldn't stop myself.

My hands gripped hers as I pounded into her.

Melasina's legs curled around me, her heels hitting my ass. Her head rolled to the side, and for the first time, she closed her eyes, looking away from me.

From us.

"Look at me," I said, in a voice I nearly didn't recognize as my own.

Slowly, she turned her head back to me and opened her eyes.

It nearly killed me, but I slowed down, and kissed her. Then I moved in and out, slowly, slowly, and with a shout, I emptied myself into her.

Melasina cried out, and her pussy clenched around me once more.

I leaned down, my forehead to hers, both of us breathing heavily. I couldn't move.

"Wow," Melasina said. She was smiling. "That wasn't what I expected when I opened the door."

"That's because you wanted to throw me out again," I grinned.

"Partly. And partly because I wanted you right where you are."

"I'm glad that side won out," I said.

"Me, too," Melasina said.

I carefully lifted myself off her. "Bathroom?" I asked.

"Through the kitchen," Melasina pointed toward the back of the house.

She was beautiful, lying on the bed naked, her skin pink and warm, mixed with cream, her hair a mess. She looked like a woman who'd just had great sex.

Which she had.

With me.

I was grinning as I walked through the kitchen. Her house was a Creole cottage, and the bathroom was off the kitchen at the back of the house. I cleaned up, and headed back to the room.

There was dirt on her tile, and I moved to the side to avoid it with my bare feet. As I did, I stepped into another little pile, and then another. I stopped, brushing my feet off, and went back to her room.

Frowning, I bent down to brush at my feet again.

"What's wrong?" Melasina asked. She'd slid under the blankets on the bed.

"There was dirt on the floor of the kitchen," I said. When I looked up, her eyes were wide, and she looked... nervous. It wasn't the look of a satisfied woman I'd seen only seconds before.

In the back of my head, a warning bell rang. Soft and faint, but it was there. And it rang. "What's wrong?" I asked.

At that moment, my phone rang. I looked down to the pile where my clothes were, and knelt down to find it. It rang twice more before I fished it out of my pocket and got it to my ear.

"Hello?" I said.

"Jasper, I'm sorry to do this to you, but you need to come in," Lavinia said.

"What's up?" I asked, standing and shaking out my pants.

"Those graves? The bodies are back."

"What else?" I asked.

"I don't know, but there's too much that's happening all at once. Delphine wants us all back at Magnolia House. We need to see what magic was cast tonight at the house."

"How did you find out about the graves?" I asked.

"I had people moving through all of the city. They reported back that two bodies were found outside of the previously disturbed crypts."

"Outside of them?" I asked, pulling on my pants, keeping my back to the bed.

"Yes. What's that noise? Are you all right?"

"I hadn't made it home yet," I said. "Just finishing up some things."

"Well, finish up and get over here."

"On my way," I said. I ended the call and slid the phone into my pocket. I reached down and got my shirt and jacket, and finished dressing before I turned around.

"Is everything all right?" Melasina asked. She still had that scared, deer-in-the-headlights expression.

"No, I have to go back to Magnolia House," I said.

She nodded.

"Um.. can I call you later?" I asked.

She nodded again. I walked over to the side of the bed and leaned down to kiss her. Her arms wrapped around me as she kissed me hungrily.

"I can't wait to see you again," Melasina whispered to my lips.

My cock jumped at the feel of her voice next to my lips. "Shit, I have to go."

Melasina let her arm slide away from me. "Then I'll see you later."

"Yes, you will."

I smiled as I let myself out. As I walked down the steps of the small porch, I noticed another clump of dirt.

Stopping, I picked it up. It was... it had an odd smell. Then I laughed at myself. "Stop it or you'll go batshit," I said. Dropping the dirt, I walked to my car. She had a courtyard. One of the best things about a courtyard, no matter how small, was having a garden.

It didn't mean anything. I was just hyped up, with the information about her mother, and then the curse with Thea.

And not to mention the best sex I'd ever had in my life. I'd never been with a woman who made me feel like she did. I wanted to give myself to her, and master her all at the same time. The feel of her under my hands, my lips, with my cock inside her—I could feel myself getting hard again.

"Settle down, old son," I said as I drove back toward Magnolia House.

When I arrived, the guard at the gate let me through. On the drive over, I'd gotten myself together. I did a quick cleaning spell just to tidy up anything I might have missed. I didn't need anyone asking about this new relationship or whatever it was. I wasn't ready to talk about it. I parked and hurried inside.

Once there, I found Lavinia standing on her own, watching a group of witches in the garden.

"What's going on?" I asked.

Lavinia turned to me, and her nose wrinkled. "What in the name of Hecate have you been doing?" she asked.

"What do you mean?"

"You smell like you got hit by a skunk," she said, covering her nose.

"What?" I asked. I'd just done a cleaning spell. I sniffed at myself. "I don't smell it."

"Well, it's there. Desiree!" She gestured at one of the witches near us.

Desiree, an older woman with strawberry blonde hair, came over. She smiled, and then her nose wrinkled.

I'll give her credit. She kept the smile on her face.

"What do you smell?" Lavinia asked.

"Well, it smells like, well..." Desiree hesitated, obviously not wanting to be rude.

"Be honest," Lavinia said.

"Skunk," Desiree said.

Lavinia turned to me, her eyebrows raised. "I wasn't lying. Thank you, Desiree," she said to the other witch.

Desiree smiled and moved away.

"What were you doing?" Lavinia asked.

"I did a cleaning spell before I came in."

"Why?"

I wasn't telling her what had happened. No way in hell. "I went to a bar," I said.

She nodded. "Did you forget how to do a cleaning spell?"

"No," I grumbled.

She eyed me, and then sighed. "All right. Hit me with it."

"What?"

"Hit me with the spell you used."

"Why?"

"Am I your boss, or am I your boss?"

"You are, but that doesn't tell me why—"

"Jasper Thibodeaux, just do it!" Her voice rose.

"All right, all right." I cast a cleaning spell for her.

Nothing happened, and then the smell hit me. "Whoa," I said.

"Skunk?" Lavinia asked.

I nodded, feeling my eyes water.

"Well, we know how the curse hit you," she said with a sigh. "It's showing up differently for everyone. I'd hoped that you hadn't been hit, but Thea's spell was too powerful. And here I was hoping she was merely being optimistic," Lavinia finished with another sigh.

"What are you talking about?"

"Have you really looked at the curse?" Lavinia asked, crossing her arms like she wasn't stinking of skunk ass.

As I did too, I supposed I shouldn't cast stones. "Nope. I haven't been thinking about it at all," I said truthfully.

"Well, the last three lines say it all." Lavinia closed her eyes and quoted,

> "I damn you to your darkest fear
> I bind you to dread's cold embrace
> Until your truth you boldly face."

"What does that mean?" I asked. I couldn't think, couldn't process it.

"What's your darkest fear?" Lavinia asked.

"What?"

She waved a hand. "Never mind that. You don't have to tell me. But you will need to figure it out. Because until you face it, your magic is fucked."

"What?"

"You've done two cleaning spells, and the recipients of both have come out smelling like the back end of a skunk. Does that seem right to you?"

"No," I shook my head, trying to process what I was hearing.

"So you need to go home, and face your fear. And when you do, your spells will work right."

"You can't be sure of this," I argued.

Lavinia rolled her eyes. She grabbed my hand and brought me to a small fire pit on the side of the garden. "Start a fire."

I looked at her, and then cast the spell for fire. Nothing happened. I cast it again, and this time, the rocks from the pit flew straight up into the air.

"Shit!" I jumped back.

"Exactly. Shit," Lavinia said. "Well, you're not going to be any good here. Go home, and get some sleep. See if you can get rid of the smell. And I'll see you at the library tomorrow. Only—" she held out a finger, "If you get rid of the smell. If not, you stay home. Got it?"

"No," I said. This couldn't be happening. Not to me.

"Listen, this is going to take some time to sort out. I've already talked to some of the witches here, and not everyone is showing signs. But those that are, it's different for everyone. So for you, Jasper, your magic is going to be off kilter until you identify your fear and face it."

"You don't know that!" I nearly shouted.

"No, I don't, but I'm taking an educated guess. Now go."

"I can—"

"Do your part by breaking your piece of the curse," Lavinia finished firmly. "We didn't realize it when she cast it, but it seems that everyone that has been affected will need to break it on their own. Damn her," she added. "It's brilliant on her part, even as it's a pain in the ass."

"Thea is a powerful witch," I agreed. "Which is why you need me here."

"No, not smelling like that. And not with your magic on the fritz. Go home. Call me when it's sorted. And by sorted," Lavinia said, "I mean you cast twenty spells a day and they all come out right."

"I don't even cast twenty spells a day now!" I protested.

"Well, start! Go, Jasper!" She shooed me away.

I watched her walk away, unable to process what had just happened. Slowly, I turned and walked out of Magnolia House. I couldn't tell if it was my imagination or not that everyone stared as I left.

The feelings from the past—no! I stopped my thoughts. No. That wouldn't happen again. I wasn't that person. That wasn't my life.

I got into my car, hoping the smell didn't get in to the cushions.

CHAPTER SEVEN

Melasina

I fell back on the bed after I heard the front door close.

"Well, that was exciting," I heard from the floor.

I sat back up. "You nearly blew it!" I said. "I had to cover for you when you made noise."

"Something hit me!" Zelda shot back. "What was I supposed to do, be quiet?"

"Yes! It's not like you have a body anymore!"

"I have a skull. If it gets broken, I'm done for," she said.

"You know that for sure?" I asked.

"Yes, *chéri*, I do." There was no doubt in her voice. "Now please take me out of the bag."

I'd had to leave Zelda in the bag to get the bodies back to St. Louis No. 1 cemetery. I'd needed her help to float them along under a concealment spell. It didn't sound like much, but it was a difficult piece of spell work to not only transport, but hide something at the same time.

We'd gotten them back, though, and apparently, just in time. I'd heard Jasper on the phone. They'd found the bodies.

I got up and threw on my tee shirt and shorts again. "Thank Goddess we moved them back," I said, taking Zelda out of the bag.

She sniffed. "Good thing you're decent again. I take it that you don't intend to marry that young man," she said.

"What are you talking about?"

"In my day, those sorts of relations were for those who married, or those about to get married. But I'm guessing that may not be the case, since you let him walk out of here without a single promise," Zelda said.

"Things are a little different," I agreed, smiling. "Besides, you didn't see anything, Zelda."

"I might be old, and lacking a body, but I know what I heard. And yes, things are different, but not for the better!" she shot back.

"I want to marry someone I love," I said. "But that's not a guarantee."

Zelda snorted. "Love. What does that do, other than make people take foolish steps?"

"Well, if you married for love, maybe they wouldn't have to take foolish steps?" I asked as I carried her toward the kitchen. "I think we left dirt in here." Looking down, I saw the dirt in a clear trail. "Shit, we did, Zelda."

"Well, clean it up." She was still frosty.

I waved a hand, intending to send the dirt toward the door to the back.

Nothing happened.

I waved my hand again.

"What are you waiting for, girl?" Zelda asked.

"I don't know," I said slowly. "I've cast it twice, and nothing is happening."

"Oh, for Goddess' sake," Zelda grumbled. "Let me."

The dirt moved itself toward the door, pushing itself into a small pile.

"There? See? What's wrong with you?"

"I don't know," I said. "Let me try again." I cast a spell to open the door.

The door didn't move.

"I'm broken," I said.

"What do you mean?" Zelda asked.

"I can't cast. Nothing I've cast since I've gotten up has worked."

"He took your magic along with your maidenhead!" Zelda shouted. "Never trust men with magic!"

"Be quiet," I hissed. "No one needs to hear your shouting. And he didn't take my maidenhead."

Zelda was silent and then asked, "But did he take your magic?"

"I don't know."

"Hmmph," she said. "No marriage, and you lose things. Nothing big, just your magic. Intimacy without promise is such a good idea."

"I don't need shade from a skull," I snapped back. "Let me think."

"He might have taken that too," she grumbled.

"Jasper didn't take anything," I said.

"Then why—" Zelda stopped.

"What?"

"The curse," she said.

"What are you talking about?"

"Last night. At the ball. Where the mischief began. You fell on him, remember? I realize he's sent you into some sort of physical haze, but you were at Magnolia House tonight, and a witch cast a spell? A curse, to be more specific?"

"Goddess, that feels like ages ago," I said. "I'd forgotten for a moment." How could I think about anything else when I'd had the night I had? I'd never met anyone like Jasper. I'd never met anyone who made my clothes fall off and made me feel nothing but fabulous about it. Not ever. He was special.

"Oh, no, he didn't take a thing from you. Not your magic, your reason, your sense," Zelda said.

"What do you have against Jasper?" I asked, forgetting that earlier today, I'd had something against him as well.

"He's a man. And women are stronger witches. They want our magic. They always do," Zelda muttered.

"That may have been true before, but men and women work together now," I said.

"Hmmph," Zelda said again. "So you think."

"We've had a man as the leader of our coven before," I turned the skull toward me. Strangely, it didn't even feel weird to be talking a skull anymore.

"Well, he wasn't ever as good as the women," Zelda said.

"That's a serious bias you've got going on," I said. "And I'm not going to argue with you. Jasper didn't steal my magic."

"Who's the elder here?" Zelda snapped. "It won't ever be you if you don't open your eyes!"

I laughed. "Oh, Zelda, it was never going to be me."

"Anyone can be an elder, if they live long enough," she said. "What do you mean?"

Setting the skull on the kitchen table, I told her the whole tale of my mother while I made a pot of coffee— the necromancy, her exile, and her death.

"No wonder you are distressed, *chéri*."

"No shit," I said.

"Was there ever any sign of the necromancy in your family prior to this?"

I shook my head, even though I wasn't sure she could see me. "No. We were model citizens."

"How odd, that it should pop up in such a manner. Normally, it takes one necromancer to train another."

A chill ran through me.

"Were you aware of your mother's friends?" Zelda asked. The question sucked although her tone was kind. It was the same question Jasper had asked. But I answered Zelda.

"No. I was ten. I was bitching about history lessons at Magnolia House and trying to practice magic on the sly."

"What did your father say?"

I laughed, although there was no humor in the sound. "My dad? He shut himself away, shamed to death over his scandalous wife."

"What about you, *chéri*?" Zelda asked quietly.

"I got a nanny, and he got a new job." My voice was flat.

"I am so sorry," Zelda said. "Your father didn't come out of his grief to care for you. So you have cared for yourself. You should be proud of yourself."

"Proud of what? I haven't done a thing! I've been so scared, so afraid to be tarred with the same brush as my mom, even though I'm always going to be tarred with that brush! I haven't done anything wrong!" I shouted, throwing up my hands and stomping over to the window to glare out into my small courtyard. "And yet the minute bodies are missing, where does the coven look? Right here at that Cormier girl. Necromancer mom, you know."

"Well, you did take the bodies," Zelda said.

"That's beside the point," I snapped. "They didn't know that."

Zelda was silent, and then she said, "Since we have returned the bodies, there is no evidence left in your home. And perhaps you are correct, the man didn't steal from you. It might have been the curse."

"I don't remember what the curse said," I told her. "How do you know it was a curse?"

"Well, you said she was banished from the coven for dark magic?"

"Yes," I'd told her as we were moving the bodies out of my shed.

"Do you think it likely she showed up to share a blessing with her former coven?"

"No," I said slowly. "You're probably right."

"Tomorrow, we need to find out the exact wording of the curse."

"Or?" I asked.

"Or I shall remain convinced that it was the pleasure of the body that has stolen away your power," Zelda said formally.

I stared at her for a moment, and then my eye caught the dirt. The same dirt that Jasper had been brushing off his feet when he came back from the bathroom. Goddess save me, I hope he didn't think anything other than I'm a crap housekeeper. I did not need him nosing around. Not when he was already asking about my mom.

And he thought she might be alive! I shook my head. I supposed the library had to take in all reports, but this one was such a whopper.

"What?" asked Zelda.

"Let's go check the laundry shed," I said, picking her up. "Jasper stepped in some of the dirt we left. Might as well get rid of it." Together with my friend the skull, I went into the shed, and Zelda used a dusting spell to get the last of the grave dirt out. Then she and I went back into the house. I poured a cup of coffee, adding in cream.

"You should sleep, *chéri*," Zelda said.

"I know, but I'm all wound up."

"Nothing that you do tonight will make a difference. The man we disagree over is not going to return—"

"How do you know?" I asked.

She made a noise that sounded like a snort.

"All right, whatever." I got up, tucking her under my arm, and went back to my room. I put the coffee on the nightstand, and went to my office to find Zelda's reliquary.

"Bring me into your room," she said.

"Why?"

"Because I don't want to be in here on my own. I've had quite enough alone time," Zelda said.

"Fine." I put her skull back in, and carried the whole thing to my room. She went on the chest on the other side of my bed.

I got into bed, and finished my coffee. Caffeine

notwithstanding, as I sat in bed going over the evening. I kept moving back and forth between the idea that my mom was alive, and the amazing sex I'd had with Jasper. It was literally the best sex ever. I mean, ever. He was thoughtful, but in control and I found that I liked it.

Normally, I hated anyone attempting to direct or control me. So much of my life had been directed by things I hadn't done, and people who weren't me. But with Jasper—something about him made me feel safe to let him be in control.

Just thinking about it made my panties wet again. I rubbed my legs together, wishing he was here for round two.

I hoped he'd call.

I hoped we'd covered our tracks with the bodies well enough.

I hoped my mom was alive.

Well, two out of three wouldn't be so bad, would it? I set the now-empty cup on the nightstand and turned out the light.

"Night, Zelda."

"Goodnight, Melasina," she said.

"Thanks for your help today."

"It was my pleasure."

We both were silent, and I felt myself drifting off to sleep.

I wasn't awake, and I wasn't asleep, but I was... aware. I was in a hallway. Creamy walls, dark wood, and paintings lined the walls. I could hear footsteps ahead of me, and I followed. We moved down, and I recognized where we were.

The crypts.

Runes both carved and burned, covered the thick wooden doors. A man in front of me held out his hand. After a long moment, the heavy wooden doors opened.

There were candles all throughout the room. In alcoves, I could see chests made of glass and gold, relics, and vials of all shapes and sizes.

The man walked through the doors, and I drifted behind. He stopped, shook himself almost like a dog coming out of the water, and looked around. I ducked behind the edge of the doorway.

After a moment, I heard his footsteps again. He moved slowly, like... like he was looking for something.

Then I heard an intake of breath, and the scrape of glass against stone. The footsteps quickened, and I ducked around the edge of the door again, hoping not to be discovered. He came out of the room, and after looking around, walked away, nearly running. He was tucking something into his coat pocket.

The heavy doors of the crypt remained open. I waited for what seemed an eternity and then walked through them. I could see the glitter of the relics throughout the crypt.

"No, *chéri,* come over here."

I went to the glass box that sat at the far end of the room.

"Take this one with you," I heard.

Nodding, I tucked the box under my arm, and turned and left the room.

I sat up, heart pounding, feeling the sweat from my —dream?—on my neck and chest. "Zelda!" I hissed.

She didn't respond.

"Zelda!" I said, louder this time.

"What?"

"You told me to take you," I said.

"What?" She was awake now.

"You told me to take you."

"You remember?"

"I do," I said, not wanting to admit I'd seen it in a dream. And I'd seen a man, who'd gone in and stolen something from the crypt before me. I didn't know him. It wasn't Jasper, or any of the men from the coven.

Then I pushed him aside. He wasn't my problem at this point.

She sighed. "I did. I was tired of being in there."

"Why didn't you ask the man to take you with him?"

"He wasn't looking for me," she said.

"How could you tell?"

"You can tell these things."

"Does that mean I was looking for you?"

"You were searching for something, Melasina. I decided that it might as well be me."

"What if it was something else?" I asked, feeling frustration rise within me. What if it was something that explained what the hell was going on with me?

"If it was something in the crypt, you would have never been allowed access to it. The things stored in the crypt are not for common usage. They are to be used only with the permission and guidance of the coven leaders, or the elders."

"Hmmph," I used the same sort of noise she'd used on me earlier.

"Nothing in there would be of use to you," Zelda said, her voice firm. "Trust me on this."

"So why'd you pick yourself?"

"Well, in truth, I was tired of being in there alone. And whatever problems you were having, I could help you."

"You were so sure?" I asked.

"Haven't I?" she replied.

"Yes, you have," I admitted.

"Good. Now go back to sleep."

"Who was the man?"

"He wasn't part of our coven. He was something... more," she said.

"What does that mean?"

"Exactly what it sounds like. Something more."

"Thank Goddess tomorrow is Saturday." I changed the subject, realizing she wasn't going to say anything more about the man.

"What does that mean?" Zelda asked.

"It means I don't have to get up. So don't go yelling unless it's an emergency."

This time, when I closed my eyes, I didn't dream. Or at least, I didn't dream of the crypt. The darkness took me and I remembered no more.

CHAPTER EIGHT

Jasper

I made my way home, sniffing audibly. I couldn't smell myself. Which was something I never thought I'd have to think. But I'd smelled Lavinia after I cast a spell on her, and she was ripe.

Which meant that I was too.

How in the fuck did you get off magical skunk stink? I had no idea.

When I got home, I stripped off my clothes, bagging them in a trash bag and tossing it out on my back porch, tightly tied.

Then I got into the shower. As the hot water hit my back, I felt the sting of small scratches. From Melasina. The thought made me smile.

LISA MANIFOLD

I climbed into bed and tried to sleep. When I woke the next morning, it felt like a dump truck had come and parked on me. I was sore and tired, and I felt like ass.

I went to the shower again, determined to scrub the stench off me. I almost used magic again before I caught myself. Last night, I'd been thinking about Talia. Today, I thought about Melasina.

She was the one good thing that had come out of last night. Although how was I going to tell anyone about her? A chill rolled through me, even as I stood in the nearly scalding shower. I knew what people thought of her, of her family. We hadn't made the grave disturbances public, and with the bodies back, there was no need to. But Melasina was still a Cormier.

And I hated to be the focus of any attention, good or bad. Especially not bad.

All my life, I'd been the good kid. The one who studied, who did all the work asked of me. I volunteered around Magnolia House, and then got an apprenticeship at the library when I was seventeen. I'd already been working and living at the library for almost two years. That was because of Talia Dumond, who had been the Head Librarian.

She'd found me, trained me, and helped me to find my place within the coven.

Unlike Melasina, who had an old, if somewhat tarnished family name, my parents were what was politely termed tacky. My mother was the witch, and she'd never stopped being a witch, although when she married my dad, she kept it under wraps. But she used magic to clean the house, and make dinner, and later, to make her drinks.

It was what had killed her. Oh, alcoholism was the listed cause of death, but I saw how she made her drinks. She'd gotten drunk, used her magic to make another one, and made it too strong. She'd taken pills. And that had been it.

My father had left long before that. He never did know she was a witch, but he knew something was off. Not quite right. Well, for his world. Not for ours. The world of the covens.

My brother Caleb was older, and he'd gone into the Navy. Which left me, at fifteen, with nowhere to go. I'd already been helping at Magnolia House, and two days before Caleb was supposed to leave for basic training, Talia had come to the house.

"What are you going to do once your brother is gone?" she asked, walking around our small shotgun shack, looking at everything but touching nothing.

"Live here. Get a job," I said. I didn't need her or anyone else prying into my life.

"I could get you a job, and a place to live. And something to study. A calling," Talia looked up at me.

"Yeah? Like what?" I asked. Life had taught me that no one gave something away for nothing.

"With me. In the coven's library," Talia said simply.

I went with her. Although in hindsight, where

would I have gone? By the time I was seventeen, I was attending college, and working with Talia on anything she happened to work on.

That's what had been bothering me about the file on Melasina's mom. I'd seen it before. I just couldn't remember where. But now, standing in the shower hoping I didn't stink, I remembered.

Talia had worked on it. She'd been working on it when I'd first come to work with her in the library.

She never let me work on it with her, of course. I was an intern, a kid. There was no way in hell I'd get to touch a case like this.

But the notes—the odd notes in the back of the file. That had been Talia's handwriting. Shit.

Shit shit shit.

I needed to go and see her. See why it was that there were people who had reported seeing Sariah Cormier to the librarians, why this file was popping back up onto the radar.

I stayed in the shower until the water ran cold. I thought about Talia, and I thought about Melasina. What would I say to her? That I knew the woman who ran your mother off? That I *helped* her? A long ago memory came to me unbidden. I was watching—oh, Goddess. I was watching Melasina's house. Well, her parents' house. I remembered seeing a small girl, with long wavy black hair, holding the hand of Sariah Cormier. And then seeing Marshall Cormier come home, and swing the little girl through the air, and kiss his wife. I sat there all night, and in the dark hours of the morning, I watched Sariah Cormier head out of her house alone, in a long, dark cloak. She went straight to a local church, and began to dig at the graves.

I'd called Talia immediately. She told me to use my phone to record Sariah, and assured me that she was on her way. Seven minutes later, as Sariah was tugging a corpse out of the coffin of the small crypt, Talia arrived. She'd strode over to Sariah and stunned her.

That was the last I'd seen of the woman. I didn't know it at the time, who she was. But now, I saw it all again, and I knew this had to be Melasina's mom.

Which meant I had to tell Melasina.

Shit.

I didn't know which fire to try and put out first.

I'd only been seventeen. I was desperate for a family, and Talia provided it. I hadn't questioned her. Who would? She was the Head Librarian. I hadn't even thought about the family I was watching, what would happen to them, to the little girl, as I recorded the woman at the graves. I'd only thought about how proud Talia would be of me.

And then I wondered how the curse had hit Melasina. What was the cure? Face your greatest fear?

Where did I start?

I feared the loss of security. Of a home, and a place to belong. Of a job. Of the ability to take care of myself.

Most of all... I shook my head and got dressed. "It

can't be that easy," I said out loud. That couldn't be it. It had to be more.

Unwilling to think about my fears any longer, I went to my messenger bag and pulled out the file. The damned file that was haunting me. I looked up Melasina's number and called her.

She answered on the first ring. "Hello?"

"Hey, it's Jasper."

"Hi," she breathed into the phone, and I wanted nothing more than to go over and spend the rest of the day making her scream, making us both scream until we were hoarse and worn out.

"I wanted to come see you today, but I have some work to do first."

"I didn't get up until late," Melasina said. "For which I think I have you to thank."

"You're welcome," I said, making my voice deep.

We both laughed, and it was the laugh of two people who had recently been naked, and would hopefully be naked again.

"What are you working on? The Magnolia House thing?" Melasina asked.

"Yes. I think we've figured out that everyone who heard Thea is cursed."

"That makes sense. It was a hell of a spell. What's the focus of the curse?" Her voice changed, and I wondered if she noticed.

"You are in trouble until you face your fear."

"Really?"

I heard it again. Yep, definitely something there.

"Yes. I figured out something had gone wrong when I did a cleaning spell on myself and my boss told me I smelled like a skunk."

There was a silence on the other end, and then Melasina burst out laughing. "I'm sorry," she said between laughs. "It's not funny, but it is!"

"It'll be funny later. I tried to do a cleaning spell on my boss," I said.

"And?"

"She smelled like a skunk, too."

"Is that what's happening to everyone?" All the laughter was gone from her voice.

"No. People at the house were having different reactions. The best guess of the librarians is that you have to face your biggest fear to put things right."

"Some people will never be the same," Melasina said.

"No, they won't. Have you noticed a change in anything?" I asked.

"Yes," she said.

"What?"

"I can't use magic."

"What?" I whispered. "Are you sure?"

"Yes. I tried to make coffee, do the dishes, do some... cleaning, and I couldn't do any of it. These aren't hard spells, either. I've known them forever."

I found myself nodding even though I knew she

couldn't see me. "I understand. I'll need to let my bosses know."

"Fine," Melasina said, and there was a definite change in her voice.

"What's wrong?" I asked immediately.

"I'm not a fan of your career choice," her voice was tight.

"Why? Oh, uh... well, that makes sense," I said, remembering Talia. It was Talia who'd singlehandedly sent her mother away. Well, not single handedly. I'd helped.

I hadn't paid attention to the details in the file when I'd first seen it. I was busy, the grave disturbances were at a really inconvenient time, I had to go pick up my suit —on and on. I didn't even remember my late night stake out until this morning. "Listen, I need to talk to you."

"I need to talk to you, too," Melasina breathed over the phone.

Everything else was forgotten. The sound of her voice, that breathy tone, made me instantly hard and I could hear my heartbeat pounding at the thought of her naked body under me.

"Put me on video," I commanded. There was something about her that made me want to take charge, to dominate.

There was a hesitation, a catch in Melasina's breath, and then she switched to the camera feature. Her hair was up in a messy bun, and she was wearing short shorts, no shoes, and a tank top with no bra. I could see her nipples through the camera.

"Let your hair down," I said.

Her mouth parted, her eyes wide, Melasina's hand went up to her hair and pulled out the band holding it up. Her dark locks tumbled around her face and down onto her breasts.

"Take off your shorts," I said, my voice husky.

The camera shook a little as she stood, and slid the shorts down her long legs. She wasn't wearing panties. "I approve of the lack of underwear," I said with a smile.

Melasina didn't reply, only smiled. That smile, her faith in me—it made me so hard it hurt.

"Why are you all dressed up?" she asked.

"What would you like to see?"

"Are you going to tell me to touch myself?" Her head dropped down and she looked up at me through her lashes.

"I was," I said.

"Then I want to see you touch yourself, too," Melasina said.

I'd never, ever done this before. I'd had a couple of girlfriends, but my work took priority, and I never felt this... adventurous. This excited.

I unbuttoned the button on my jeans, and then unzipped them slowly. I pushed down my briefs, and my cock sprang free. "Is this what you wanted to see?" I said.

"Yes," Melasina nodded, her voice a purr. "I'm

showing you mine. I want you to show me yours." She drew a finger between her legs.

My cock throbbed in response and I had to stop myself from groaning.

She dragged her fingers across her pussy, a small moan escaping her.

I took my cock in my hand, giving it a few strokes. I wasn't going to last long if—

"The chickens! The chickens are loose!" A woman's voice from what sounded like somewhere in the house, shrieked at air siren volume.

Melasina's head jerked up as though she'd been shot, and she dropped the phone.

"Shit!" I heard her swear, and there was a rush of footsteps. Then the phone was picked up, and Melasina was tugging on her shorts with one hand. "I'm sorry, Jasper, my neighbor, Zelda—she's old, and she—I'm coming," she yelled. She looked back down at the camera. "I'm really sorry. Can I have a rain check?"

"Yes, you can," I said.

Before I could say anything else, make something of the clusterfuck that had just occurred, she hung up.

Right now, I could wring Zelda's neck right along with the damn chickens. Well, hell. I stood up, tucking myself back in. Zelda's steam whistle shriek had effectively killed all my sex mojo. Probably for the best. I had things to do.

But then, I was going to see Melasina, and I was

going to tell her the truth. About Talia, and me, and the part I'd played in the exile of her mother.

And I was going to hope for the best.

First, however, I needed to go see Talia. The notes in the back of Sariah's file had to be clarified. If I was going to risk whatever this was with Melasina, I needed to be sure.

CHAPTER NINE

Melasina

"Zelda! What in the hell are you doing?" I'd moved Zelda into my office, setting her reliquary on the desk. So she could look out the window. Which meant I was probably going insane, but whatever. I'd already graduated to grave robbing. Might as well go all in, right?

Turning the reliquary around, I glared at the skull. "You want to explain what that was all about?"

"You're already short on magic," she said, not at all repentant. "And you're going to go give more of it to some magic man? I don't care what he does to you, it's not worth your magic!"

"He's not stealing my magic!" I shouted back. "That's already gone!"

"After you gave yourself to him. Like you were about to again."

"Yeah, and it would have been great," I muttered, crossing my arms. "You can't keep doing that. I like Jasper. I can't see where we could go if you keep shouting about chickens."

"The little death is indeed marvelous, but it is fleeting," Zelda said.

"The little death?" I asked.

"The completion, the place where the sky explodes around you," she said. If she had been standing in front of me, I would have bet she was grinding her teeth.

"Oh, orgasm."

"Yes, the completion. When you orgasm," she spoke the unfamiliar word slowly, "You are open as you are no other time. Your spirit, your magic, your very soul is vulnerable and on display."

"That's kind of part of the point," I said.

"That's when they steal it," she insisted.

"What the hell happened to you?" If I was remembering my history correctly, Zelda Dupuis had never married. Never had children, although she'd taken in many during her time as the leader of our coven. One of my ancestors had a claim to her in that fashion.

"I fell in love. His name was Ronan. Ronan Dhu, Ronan the Black, for he was a tall, dark man, much like your own." Her voice sounded distant.

"And he asked me to consummate our love, to pledge ourselves to one another. He was a Druid, a man of magic from the isles, and when he talked, his voice could carry me to green pastures in another world."

"What did you do?" I asked.

"I agreed. What else would I do? My parents approved, even though he was Irish, not French. He was a Druid, and a scholar, and a man of repute." She stopped.

A feeling of overwhelming sadness came over me. It wasn't mine—it was Zelda's.

"We met one night, under the full moon. He insisted. He wanted to see me by moonlight," Zelda said. "And we spoke words that bound us, and then I let my dress fall. I was wearing nothing underneath—not stays, petticoats, nothing. He stared at me in the moonlight, and lay me down upon the furs he'd brought." She stopped.

When she spoke again, her voice had lost the dreamy tone of memory. "Well, you know what happened next. As we reached the completion, and I cried out for him, I felt a hand reach inside of me."

"What?" I asked, trying to picture this.

"No, not a physical hand. It was a cold shadow hand that reached beneath my heart. I looked up to see his face, and Ronan, the man who'd just pledged himself to me, was directing a shadow toward me, even as he proclaimed his loved for me. The hand tugged at me, and I knew it was trying to take my magic. The tugging was on my magical soul. I'd never believed in such a thing," Zelda said. "But that night, I felt it."

"What did you do?"

"I shoved at him with all my might, calling on the Goddess to give me her strength. He flew from me, and got to his knees, his mouth open and twisted in a snarl of anger. 'Give it to me!' he shouted, and he pointed at me. The shadow I'd seen below my heart came toward me with the swiftness of a snake. I sent a wall of flame toward him, tears streaming down my face. Then I cast a holding spell, and when the flames died down, I could see him, naked, arm still thrown up toward me."

"Oh, Zelda," I said.

"I dressed, crying as I did so. I cloaked him, for even as a young girl, I was skilled. I was already training then to be the High Priestess. I brought him to my home, and my parents... well, suffice to say my parents were not happy that I'd given myself to him before marriage. They were even less so when they'd learned of his deception."

"What happened to him?" I asked.

"He was stripped of his magic, which is the punishment for one who would steal magic from another. Our bond was broken. I lost a piece of myself, as is appropriate. His memory was erased, and he was sent back to Ireland to live the life of a normal, fallen man."

"I'm so sorry," I said.

"I was ruined. No one would have me, not after I'd given myself to him. Not only that I'd given myself to someone I wasn't yet married to, but everyone knew. And I was questioned, for I had not seen his true nature."

"I understand that," I said, thinking of my life since my mother left.

"But I kept my magic, *chéri*. He did not succeed, and I rose to become all that I was supposed to be."

"I don't think that's Jasper's end goal," I said.

"I would have fought to the death defending Ronan," she replied. "Perhaps you are right. Things are different. You are not ruined by allowing a man close, and that's something good, to my way of thinking. But that doesn't mean men are any better. There are always men—and women—who would steal what is not theirs."

"Have you seen that?" I asked.

"Many times," her voice was sad. "I want to protect you, Melasina."

"Why?" I asked.

"Because you are a member of my coven. Of my family. I will not see harm come to you."

"Even as I'm digging up bodies?" I asked.

"Even then. You are not your mother," she replied.

I sat down, thinking about all she'd said. "I think my magic loss is due to the curse Thea threw down on us at the ball," I said.

"I would agree, but I would have you be careful. Jasper is skilled with his body," she said, her voice grave.

The words gave me the giggles. I covered my mouth

to try and stop them, because I didn't want her yelling at me. He was very skilled with his body. And there was something in his voice, his manner that spoke to something deep inside me.

I'd spent so much of my life being careful, being so controlled, so perfect. I didn't put a toe out of line, because I feared what would happen if I did. But with Jasper? I wanted to be out of control. I wanted to allow him to lead me to all the dark, sweaty, places where it was just the two of us. Giving, taking, and each other. Nothing more.

I could see that with him. "I'll be careful. No more chickens, all right?" I asked.

She sighed. "Very well. You know, now, and you are warned. Do you have a spell that could cast him from you?"

"Um, no magic?" I waggled my fingers at her. "Remember?"

"You are defenseless," she grumbled. "What timing."

"We'll figure something out," I said. "But what if it's the curse? What was it you said? You have to face your greatest fear?" I couldn't remember what it was that Thea had shouted.

"You young witches. What has happened to memorizing what you hear?" Zelda said. "I remember the pertinent lines.

I damn you to your darkest fear

I bind you to dread's cold embrace
Until your truth you boldly face,"

she chanted. "That's the part where she drops the curse on you. You have to face your darkest fear. That's if the man hasn't stolen your magic."

"Jasper told me that other witches are experiencing problems. He can't do magic correctly."

"What does that mean?"

I started to laugh. "It means he did a cleaning spell on himself and came out smelling like a skunk."

After a moment, Zelda joined me. "That's funny," she said. "And he is not the only one?"

"No, it's happening to witches who were there when Thea showed up."

"All right. I'll go along with the idea that this is Thea's doing. What is your deepest fear?"

"I don't know, Zelda! I have so many!"

"That could be it then," she said. "Fear itself."

"What are you, my shrink?"

"I have no idea what that is, so no."

I threw up my hands. "This isn't helping."

"Then go do something else, and leave me here in peace."

"Fine!" I shouted, stomping out of the room.

I spent the rest of the day cleaning, and I went grocery shopping, steadfastly ignoring the skull in the glass box in my office.

After I'd made dinner, and stared at the TV without really watching it, my phone rang.

"Hello?"

"It's me, Jasper. Can I come by?"

He sounded all out of sorts.

"Sure," I said, getting up. "When should I—"

"I'll be there in half an hour," Jasper said. He hung up.

"Well," I said to the empty room.

"What does that mean?" Zelda called from my office.

I walked in to see her. "Jasper is coming over. I'll leave the door open, so you can listen. I need to drape a scarf or something over your box. I'm sure he'd recognize you, and I'm not ready for that yet."

"Can't wait to get rid of me?"

"No, actually, despite your pig headedness this afternoon," I said stiffly. "But I haven't figured out how to sneak you back in."

She made a noise. I wasn't sure what she was trying to convey, but I was going with not positive. Rather than argue, I went to my room and found a gauzy pink scarf. I draped it over the reliquary, and left the door open to the office. Then I went to my bathroom and primped a little. I was hoping we'd finish what we'd started earlier today. The thought of his mouth on me, his cock pounding into me—it made my nipples tighten and my sex wet. I wanted him in the worst way.

Which wasn't like me at all, but I didn't want to look

too closely, to question. I was afraid if I did, it would all disappear.

"Is that my worst fear?" I asked my reflection in the mirror. "I'm afraid I'll lose him?" Jasper was such a piece of being normal. A good looking man, who wanted to be with me, like I saw with so many couples in our coven. I'd been afraid for a long time no one would want me, that I'd always be alone.

"Is that it?" I whispered. I stared at myself. Nothing happened. I didn't look one bit different.

I cast a spell to move the dirt out of the bathroom.

Nothing happened.

I tried to pull back the shower curtain from around the claw footed tub.

The curtain didn't move.

I cast a spell to turn off the light.

It was bright as mid-afternoon in my bathroom. The light stayed on.

"Well, hell," I said. I finished brushing my teeth, and went to wait for Jasper.

Two weeks later

In the two weeks that we'd been seeing each other, Jasper and I hadn't managed to make it back to bed together. Not once. Not at all. Every time we came close, something happened.

That first night he came over, I could tell that he was upset.

"What's going on?" I asked.

"I just came from my mentor," he said.

"And?" I wasn't connecting the dots.

He shook his head, sitting down next to me on the sofa. One thing led to another and just as he carried me into my room and put me on the bed, his phone rang.

"Don't answer it," I begged.

"It's my work ringtone," he said.

Within five minutes, he was out the door. The effects of the curse was making its way around our coven, and his boss needed his help.

Every night since then, he'd come over. In that time, I caught dinner on fire. Twice. The water hose under my sink popped off, and we spent ten minutes splashing around in water.

Then his car broke down on the way to my house. He took it to his mechanic the next day, and there was nothing wrong.

Then he got a flat tire. Then I got a flat tire.

Then my car broke down. Although that was my heater hose popping off, so at least there was a reason.

We weren't able to have sex, which was what we both wanted to do. We both laughed a lot, and talked, but there wasn't a lot of involvement when we were both dealing with one crisis after another.

Still, I was enjoying myself. And the promise of wonderful for when we were able to get back to bed—

oh, that thought had given me some very detailed dreams.

Finally, he called. "I can't come by tonight."

"Oh, no, what happened?" I asked.

"I have to work," Jasper said.

There was something in his voice, something that... I couldn't pinpoint it, but he wasn't being completely straight with me. "I'm sorry," I said. "I wanted to see you."

"I don't want your house to burn down if I show up," he said.

"Well, there is that, but what else could happen?" I asked.

"I'll call you tomorrow," Jasper said, and he ended the call.

"Not coming over?" Zelda asked.

"No, he has to work."

"They always do," she said. "No, no, don't start. I'm glad he's not coming over. I want to talk to you."

"About?" I found that I was dispirited. Through the last two weeks and every fucking bad instance of Murphy's Law, I thought it was just a thing. Something we could laugh over. But I'd heard something different in his voice tonight.

"I hate to admit that I am wrong, but a good leader does so, no matter how painful," Zelda said.

"What do you mean?" I asked.

"This is the curse, Mel," she said. She'd started calling me Mel. And she'd told me not to worry about getting her back. She didn't want to go back. I figured I had enough problems, although I knew that the fact the reliquary was missing was a big concern for the coven. Jasper had mentioned it.

I had no idea how I was going to tell him about Zelda. Or my part in busting her out. And keeping her.

"What do you mean?"

"What is your darkest fear?"

"I—"

"Don't give me that. I know you've been considering it. I know I have. What is it? This will be your life—no magic, no man, no happiness, no moving forward—until you face that fear."

"I hope Thea falls in a bayou," I muttered. "With gators."

"Be that as it may, you're wearing the curse. You'll do so until you break it. It's time to face your fear," Zelda said.

CHAPTER TEN

Jasper

The past two weeks had been torture. Not only because every piece of bad luck—my momma would have said bad karma—I'd ever gathered had hit, but because I was keeping something from Melasina.

Two weeks ago, I'd gone to see Talia. She'd retired because she'd gone blind. She lived in a house near the library, and she had witches from our coven that came over and helped her. She might be blind, but she was still able and strong. She just couldn't read, and she didn't want others to read to her. She'd put herself into retirement.

We would have let her stay as long as she wanted.

A young witch, not yet at her majority, opened the door when I knocked.

"Is she up for visitors?" I asked the girl.

"I'm always up to see you, Jasper Thibodeaux," I heard from further back in the house.

I smiled, and the witch let me pass. She followed me into the kitchen, where Talia sat at a small table, sipping a cup of tea.

"I'm going to do the shopping, Miz Dumond," she said.

"You have the list?" Talia asked.

"Yes, ma'am," the girl said.

"All right. I'll see you when you get back. Jasper will be here while you're gone."

I waited until I heard the front door slam. "You don't really need someone here all the time," I said.

"No, but it makes the coven feel good to help, and it's a good thing for the younger witches to do. We do some spell work, and some potion mixing."

"You haven't really retired," I said with a smile.

She reached across the table and patted my hand, finding it easily without sight. "No, and I never shall. What brings you to me today?"

"You heard about Thea? Her curse at the annual ball?"

She nodded. "Were you there?"

"I heard it. I was knocked down by the force of it," I admitted.

"How is it manifesting?"

"It's different for everyone," I said. "My magic is backwards. If I cast a spell the opposite thing will happen. Usually in the worst way possible," I said.

"What else?"

"I have a friend who cannot cast at all."

"A friend?" Talia asked, smiling. Her eyes crinkled as she smiled, turning her face to me.

"Yes, a friend. That's all she is. She might be more."

"I'll leave you be," she patted my hand again. "But she's sure she can't cast?"

"She's been trying ever since the ball."

"And nothing?"

"Nope. Not a thing."

"What's your deepest fear?" Talia asked.

"You heard about that?"

"I hear everything, my dear boy."

"I don't know," I stood up, feeling restless. "What do you think?"

"I can't answer that," Talia said. "If I do, it will be my idea of your deepest fear. Not yours. No, only you can answer that."

"What does that mean, face it?" I asked, referring to the curse.

"I suppose it means you have to do the thing that scares you the most. But that's not the thing that brought you here," she said, her sightless eyes searching my face.

I felt like she could see me. I sat down, and pulled

out my messenger bag. "You're right as always, Talia. I have some questions about a file."

"What are they? Who is the file about?"

"Sariah Cormier," I said.

"That woman," Talia muttered. "Is she back? I heard that there were graves disturbed. Have you spoken to her daughter?"

"How did you hear that?" I asked, leaning back in my chair. "Lavinia and I kept it quiet. There were graves disturbed, but the bodies were returned, and no harm was done."

"That's what you know," Talia said, her mouth twisting in a sneer. "It just takes one of those creatures to wreak havoc on a coven."

"Wait," I said. "What did you mean?"

"What are you talking about?"

"You asked me if she was back," I said slowly. "That was your handwriting in the notes."

A strange expression crossed Talia's face. Then her features settled into the calm, determined look I'd seen on it a thousand times. "I haven't made any notes about Sariah Cormier."

"There are notes in this file," I opened it up to the last two pages. "Notes that give an address, that say, Confined, and then there are two further notes that state the person submitting them is sure they saw her. There was a request to go and see, to see if was her. To see what it was that caused people concern. And those notes, Talia," I leaned forward, "at the end of each report from a member of our coven, are marked, Dismissed." I leaned back.

She didn't speak.

"Also in your handwriting."

"You don't know that," she said. Her voice was steady as she took a sip of her tea.

"Talia, I worked with you for eight years. I know your handwriting as well as I know my own."

"What is it you think you see, Jasper?"

"Sariah Cormier is alive," I said.

The corner of her mouth twitched, but Talia didn't reply.

"You exiled her, and allowed everyone, her husband, her daughter—to think she was dead."

"Nonsense. Why would I do that?"

I watched her. Something was off. She was too calm. She'd been prepared for this. Maybe not from me but she knew, at some point, she would be asked about this.

"You tell me," I said.

"There is nothing to tell. Sariah Cormier was seen attempting to rob a grave. As you yourself saw," she tapped my hand for a third time. "After we had several graves that were robbed before you caught her. She was your prize, Jasper. Did you share that with her daughter? I'm assuming you spoke with the Cormier girl. Like mother, like daughter, you know."

"No, I don't know," I said. "That's why I am asking you. What does this mean?" I tapped the file. "Why is there an address attached to this? In Arkansas? Why were these eyewitness reports dismissed? Why was there no follow-up?"

She didn't speak.

My horror grew. I knew I was right, even as Talia refused to speak.

"I did my job," Talia said. "That is what I did." She shrugged, but it was deliberate. Practiced. "You need to do yours." She pushed back from the table. "Now, I believe I'm tired, Jasper," she said. She stood, and moved gracefully through the kitchen, turning to the right toward a room. She walked into the room and shut the door.

I left her house unsure of what I'd heard, other than lies.

Was Melasina's mother alive?

Had she been unfairly accused?

It felt like I had the tip of a ball of yarn, and it was stuck somewhere that I couldn't see.

For the next two weeks, in between being frustrated with Melasina, I tried to find someone to verify that the address listed in the file was occupied. Or to get a picture. But the witch I sent wasn't able to gather any further info.

"There's someone there," she said, when she came back to New Orleans after four days. "I see the curtains move, but they don't come out."

"Not at all?" I asked.

The witch, named Nadia, shook her head. Red curls bounced as her head moved. "No. And I showed up at all hours."

"Someone's being careful," I said.

"What are you looking for?" she asked.

"I'm not sure," I said truthfully. "Just following a lead I found in an old file."

"Does it have anything to do with Thea's curse?"

"Sadly, no," I said. "How are you affected?"

"I can only do earth spells."

"Oh," I said. "All my magic is backwards."

Nadia smiled at me. "This sucks. You figure out your fear?"

"No," I said. "I have some ideas, but I haven't gotten further than that."

"She sure did a number on us," Nadia said.

"Well, it was clever to have the curse affect everyone differently," I said.

"Yeah. I can't wait to get my shit sorted. Sorry," she looked up. "Is there anything else you need?"

I shook my head.

"Then I'm going to go home and... well, whatever," Nadia said. With a wave of her hand, she left.

Every night, I went to Melasina's. By some unspoken agreement, we didn't go out. We didn't meet at a café for coffee. We didn't go grab a bite for dinner. We met at her house. And every night, something happened. We hadn't been able to be with one another since the first time. There weren't even any crazy neighbors with chickens.

It was just life.

Which to me was fate.

Which meant I needed to face my fear.

I called her. "I have to work," I said. "I'll call you tomorrow." I needed a break. The hope of being with her, of being able to take our relationship further, and then seeing my hopes dashed, was wearing.

Not to mention, I was keeping a secret.

"My fear," I said out loud.

I spent the rest of the night figuring out which fear was bigger, and how I was going to make this right.

I needed my magic back to normal. I needed to tell the truth.

And I needed Melasina.

We hadn't spent that much time together, but I knew. This was the woman I was supposed to be with. I'd known it since she'd opened the door and shaken my hand the first time I met her.

The next morning, I was up early, and I called her.

"Hi!" Melasina sounded cheerful.

"I have to go out of town," I said. "I'll be a couple of days at the most. Then I want to talk to you when I get back."

She sighed, and I heard an entire conversation in that sigh. "Jasper, if you don't want to see me anymore, just tell me. There's no need for an elaborate thing."

"That's not it at all, Mel," I said.

"Why do you call me that?" she asked.

"What?" I replied.

"Mel, when did you start calling me Mel?"

I shrugged. "I don't know. It just fits you. Why?"

"I haven't heard you call me that before. So. You were saying? A couple of days?"

"Yes. I have something I need to check out, and it's out of town."

Mel sighed again. "All right. I'll hopefully see you when you get back."

"You will," I promised.

"OK," she said.

Mel hung up.

OK. That felt bad. But I had to do this. I had to see this through, no matter what happened. If I wanted a future in this coven, as a witch, with Mel—this had to be done.

"Face your fear," I said. "Face your fear."

I grabbed my backpack and headed out the door. I had a long drive ahead of me.

~

Seven hours later, I was on the outskirts of Hot Springs, Arkansas. I had an address outside of the downtown area, by the lake. I'd Googled it, and it was a small, older cottage. I found myself nervous and excited at the thought of what I might find, and nervous about what I might not find.

My phone rang.

"Hello?"

"Where are you?" Lavinia's voice rang through my car.

"I'm in Arkansas."

"Do I want to know?" Lavinia asked. "Wait, no, I don't want to know. Here's the thing. Melasina Cormier, you know, the one I had you question?"

"Yes," I said slowly.

"She's asked for a full coven elders meeting tomorrow night. So whatever it is you're doing, and I trust you, even with your ass backwards magic, get yourself back here. I want the entire library staff on deck."

"You should bring Talia," I said.

"Are you serious?" Lavinia asked.

"Completely." One way or the other, I was going to drag this into the light.

I hoped I was doing the right thing. I thought I was, but sometimes it was hard to see when you were in the middle of things. Regardless, this was something that had to be fixed. It fell to me, and I didn't have a choice. I would fix this.

And let the chips fall where they may.

CHAPTER ELEVEN

Melasina

*J*iggled my foot as I sat in the kitchen, trying to finish my coffee.

"Stop," Zelda said. "You're making me nervous."

"I can't help it," I said. "I'm so scared I think I might throw up."

"Well, please do so now. You will not help your case if you cast up your accounts all over the feet of the coven leadership."

"You're so helpful," I snarled at Zelda.

"Yes, I am. You just can't see it."

"What if this doesn't work?" I asked for what felt like the millionth time.

"It will," she said.

"You've been out of the loop for a while."

"That doesn't take away what I know," Zelda was calm.

Which made me want to throw her box across the room.

But instead, I stood, and placed the box in the biggest bag I had, which was a beach bag made of brightly colored straw. I walked to the door, stopping to check my hair once more. I'd pulled it back in a sleek chignon, and I was dressed in cute flats, a black skirt, and a black button up shirt.

I wore my mother's gold earrings, and the pendant that Jasper had brought back to me. Other than that, I was plain. Almost severe.

But the less attention I called to myself, the better, I felt.

I put the bag carefully in the car, and buckled it in.

"Much safer than when you brought me home," Zelda said.

"You think this is home?" I asked.

"You think the crypt was home?" She gave a laugh that sounded a lot like a hoot. "Come on, girl. You've only lost your magic, not your wits."

"Oh, Jasper didn't steal that, too?" I teased.

"He's stolen something," she muttered.

I ignored her as I pulled up to the gate at Magnolia House. I'd asked Delphine if I could drive here, because I really wasn't trying to trot all the way over with Zelda in my arms. She'd agreed, more out of curiosity, I thought. I didn't care.

As I got out of the car, and moved around to take out Zelda, I could feel the eyes watching from the house. I went to the door, and Delphine herself opened it.

"Welcome," she said. She narrowed her eyes as she looked me over, stopping at the beach bag. "Interesting choice of bag."

"Yes, it is," I said.

"Come in. We're waiting for you." She closed the door behind me, and then led me off to the right. Beyond the kitchen, there was a room that had been built onto the back of the house, and it was here that all the leaders of my coven were gathered.

Delphine walked in and I stopped, taking a deep breath. Then I followed her.

Delphine took a seat at the head of the ring of chairs. "You have asked to see us, Melasina Cormier. We are here. We will always be here for our members. So tell us, why have you called us?"

I looked around. It looked like all the librarians were here—my eyes narrowed as I saw Talia Dumond, the woman who had pursued my mother mercilessly. She'd visited our home, and I remembered her arguing with my mother. When my mother was exiled before the entire coven, Talia had stood watching, not saying a world, a smile upon her face.

Now she was blind. I hoped she choked on what I had to say.

Jasper was in the second row of chairs that lined the left and right of the room. He smiled at me, the white of his teeth gleaming momentarily. I felt heartened seeing him, even though I was probably shooting any hope of us in the foot. That was all right—well, it wasn't, not really, but I had to do this.

A hooded figure sat next to him. I smiled briefly, and turned my attention back to Delphine.

"I know that the curse has affected all of us differently. But we all need to face our fears, and I have figured out that this is my greatest fear. I must accept who I am, and do so publicly." I took another deep breath. "I am the daughter of Sariah Cormier. She was exiled for necromancy from this coven. I never saw any sign of such a practice during my life with her, but I cannot change the past. I've always been careful, ever since Talia Dumond insured my mother's exile."

A hiss of whispers followed my words. Talia herself stared straight ahead.

"Because I didn't want to suffer the same fate. I felt that if I did everything right, I'd be seen for myself." I sighed. "That hasn't happened. I am, and will always be, Sariah Cormier's daughter. She was a necromancer. A little over a month ago, I began to experience strange things. And three weeks ago, I woke up to scratches on my hands and dirt under my fingers."

There was an audible gasp.

"Like mother, like daughter, indeed," Talia spoke,

her voice dripping with anger. "We've heard enough. I call for an exile of Melasina Cormier."

"No," another voice spoke up. It was Jasper. "Delphine, I ask that you listen to what Melasina has to say, and then that I be allowed to speak before you make a decision."

"What is there to discuss?" Talia scoffed.

I was watching Jasper, and the hooded figure next to him stirred.

"She has admitted that she is continuing her mother's evil ways. Let us be done," Talia continued.

"Please," I said. "I'll accept your decision, but I want to be allowed to finish."

The room went silent as all eyes turned to Delphine. "Melasina, you may continue. After you are done, we will hear you, Jasper Thibodeaux."

Talia made a dismissive noise.

"I didn't know why this was happening, because I couldn't remember anything," I said. "I went to clean my nails, and I heard shouting out in my shed. I went into the garden, and there were two bodies on the floor."

More gasps. Delphine held up a hand.

"And sitting on the washer was this," I bent down and took Zelda and her reliquary out of my beach bag.

There were shouts, and people stood up, hands waving. Delphine stood, and held out her hands. "Enough," she thundered. "Melasina, how did you come to have our founder in your possession?"

"I'm not just a box," Zelda said. "And I would appreciate it if you would hear the girl out." Her words carried a ring of power that silenced a lot of the whispering.

Talia was staring at the reliquary, her face taut and angry.

"I am not sure," I said. "I had a dream one night where I was walking into the crypt, and I was behind a beautiful man. He opened the doors, and took something of glass, and then ran away. But he left the doors open, and I went in. Zelda called out to me, and I brought her home with me."

"Is this true?" Delphine asked Zelda.

"It is. The handsome man did come in, and steal a vial from a red pillow. Then Mel came in, and I told her to take me."

"Why would you do that?" Delphine asked.

"My reasons are my own," Zelda said with the manner of a queen. "The point is, I concur with the girl's story."

Delphine stared at Zelda for a long moment, and then turned her gaze back to me. I couldn't read her face. "Do you have more to say?" she asked me.

"I do, if you don't mind."

She gestured at me to continue.

"I have been trying to figure out why I was walking in my sleep. Why I came to the crypt. Why I had bodies in my laundry shed. Once I found the bodies and Zelda, she helped me to get the bodies back to St. Louis No. 1

the night of the ball. And I tried to work out how to bring her back. In that, she wasn't very helpful." I glared down at Zelda.

"No, I was not," Zelda sniffed.

One of the witches to the left of Delphine covered her mouth with her hand, making a choking sound. Which suggested that she was familiar with Zelda.

"So I am returning her to where she belongs. I am asking for your forgiveness for not doing so before. I am confessing that I was the person who removed and returned the bodies. And I am asking for help to discover why it is I have been doing these things." I stopped, and let the breath I didn't know I'd been holding out.

"This is rubbish!" Talia got up, pointing at me. "This is—"

"Talia, sit down," Delphine said.

Talia stopped in mid-rant, and sank back into her chair.

I managed not to smirk. She couldn't see me anyway.

"How long have you been sleep walking?" Delphine asked.

"I don't know," I said. "But I woke up with dirty hands and dressed in my clothes and with shoes from time to time a little over a month ago to when Zelda came to my home."

"Has she sleep walked since you've been there?" Delphine asked Zelda.

"No," Zelda said. "I watched, each night. I also put a ward over her home, so that might have stopped someone or something that was affecting her."

Delphine nodded, and reached out her hands to the witches on either side of her. There were four on each side who clasped hands. They all closed their eyes.

The room was completely silent. I risked a glance at Jasper. He was smiling, almost as if he was proud of me. As I turned my gaze back to Delphine, I saw Talia. She was glaring in a manner that would have killed me if her eyes had daggers.

Delphine opened her eyes. "We have discussed your situation. You have come to us to seek help, to your sisters and brothers, as you should. I do not sense untruth in your words. And the founder, Zelda Dupuis, stands with your account. So my decision is thus: We will help you discover why you're walking in your sleep, and you have our thanks for your care of Zelda." Delphine nodded to a witch off to the right, and the man hurried over, bending down and reaching for Zelda.

"No!" Zelda shouted. "I have more I wish to say."

The witch stopped, his hands outstretched, and he looked to Delphine. Her eyebrow went up, and she nodded to the witch, who returned to his seat. "You are always free to speak, Zelda."

"I want to stay with Melasina Cormier," Zelda said clearly. "I prefer to be with the members of our coven rather than locked away in a crypt. I am always available to the leadership for anything they might need but I request that my resting place be one that I find more pleasing."

"No," Talia rose again. "This is not right! She's a necromancer! The daughter of a filthy necromancer! How do none of you see it?" She threw her hands in the air.

"I would like to speak," Jasper said.

Delphine frowned. "Is there anyone who doesn't wish to speak at this very moment?"

Wisely, everyone remained silent.

She sighed. "What is it you feel you must say, Jasper?"

"I would like to refute Talia's claims," Jasper strode to the center of the room, standing about a foot from me. "We did, as she says, see Sariah Cormier seeking a corpse from a grave. And Sariah was exiled. But she is not dead. And Talia knows it."

"He is mad," Talia spat, crossing her arms.

Jasper looked to the left, and the hooded figure that was sitting next to him stood, and drew back the hood.

"I am Sariah Cormier," my mother said in a soft voice. "And I'm very much alive."

There was a moment of silence, and then the room burst into noise so loud that I wanted to cover my ears. But I only had eyes for my mother.

She stepped out from the second row of seats and came over to me. "Is it really you, Mellie?" she asked softly.

I took her outstretched hands in my own. "Is it really you?"

Tears fell down her cheeks as she nodded.

"How?" I asked.

"Jasper found me," she said, turning to smile at Jasper.

"Jasper, explain yourself," Delphine said loudly.

I pulled my mother close, putting my arm around her waist and standing over Zelda's reliquary. The feeling in the room was high, and I didn't want her getting knocked around or stepped on.

"Well, I didn't see that coming," Zelda said. "Is that really Momma Grave Digger?"

"Zelda!" I said. "Not the time!" I looked up to see Delphine watching me, rather than Jasper. I smiled, hoping I wasn't making my situation worse.

"I found notes in the Cormier file," Jasper was saying. "Initially, I had no doubts of Sariah's guilt. I followed her that night. I saw her," he looked over to me, and I could see the apology in his eyes.

He'd seen her? He followed her? He'd said that before, but his words sunk in now.

"But in the last three years, there have been two reports of witches in our coven who felt they saw Sariah in Arkansas. Both were dismissed, with no reports of follow-up. I also found an address in the back of the file. In Arkansas." The room went still.

"I asked Talia about it, and she claimed no knowledge. So I went to Arkansas, and found Sariah Cormier, living at the address listed in the file. When I found Sariah, she didn't recognize her name. I convinced her to come back with me, since my magic is still not working correctly and asked a friend to search her memory, to see if she'd been living under a spell. And she was. A spell put on her by Talia Dumond."

"What? You'd believe that filthy woman over me?" Talia shouted. "What in the world would I gain by casting a spell over her?"

"It wasn't what you gained," Mom said. "It was about taking away from me. You wanted Marshall. But he chose me. And even after ten years, after we'd built a life, had a child together, you couldn't let it go."

"What are you inferring, Sariah?" Delphine asked.

"I'm not inferring anything. I'm stating a fact. Talia Dumond used magic against me. She enchanted me so that I would behave in a manner that would insure my exile. And then she took my memory, and let my husband and daughter believe that I was dead."

"What proof do you have?" Delphine asked.

"The woman who found her memory," Jasper spoke up.

"She is willing to speak?" Delphine asked.

"She is waiting outside," Jasper said.

"This is madness," Talia shouted.

Delphine waved a hand. Talia went completely still. "Remove her," Delphine said. "Make sure she is well bound, so that there is no chance of escape. She has much to answer for."

The witch who'd reached for Zelda and another woman walked to Talia, and took her arms. Using magic, they lifted her from the ground and towed her away.

As she left, I turned from her. I'd never think about that bitch again. Ever. I hugged my mother. "I can't believe you're here."

"Neither can I, Mellie-bean."

"Melasina and Sariah Cormier," Delphine said. We both looked at her. "You may both go home, to Melasina's home. You will not leave New Orleans. There is more to be said, much more more. We will need to speak again. But for now, you may leave. Is that acceptable to you?"

I nodded, tears forming in my eyes. I didn't see this happening, ever. It seemed like a dream. I didn't want to wake up.

My mom was here. Alive. Jasper had found her.

After he helped to send her away.

"We will also be speaking with you about your sleep walking, Melasina. Although I venture to say that Talia may be able to offer some insight into that matter, after a time," Delphine continued. "If all that has been said is accurate."

"And Zelda?" I asked. My bony friend had been very quiet, and I could tell that she was worried she wouldn't be allowed to do what she wanted. So I had to speak for her. As she'd spoken for me.

Delphine sighed, leaning back in her chair. "I will

allow Zelda Dupuis to reside with you. The elders of this coven are to have access to her as needed, as long as we are considerate of the fact that she is in your home."

"We won't see much of them," I heard Zelda mutter. I nudged the reliquary with my toe. She needed to shut the hell up right now.

"I can agree to that," I said, smiling.

"Then you may leave," Delphine said.

I put Zelda back in the bag, and carefully hitched it over my shoulder. Holding hands with my mother, I turned.

"Mel," Jasper spoke behind me. I turned slowly. I didn't want to jostle Zelda, and honestly, I wasn't sure what I wanted to say to him, if I wanted to say anything at all.

"Delphine, I want to be clear that if this coven decides, in the end, to ask the Cormiers to leave, that I be allowed to leave with them." Jasper's voice rang out through the room.

"Why?" Delphine asked.

"Because I'm supposed to be with Melasina. And I am facing my fear of not doing the right thing, of doing the wrong thing, and being honest with myself rather than what I think I'm supposed to do. Had I spoke up earlier, some of this current suffering might have been avoided. Maybe not, but I didn't speak up." He took a step toward me and lowered his voice. "I'm doing what I want to do, the right thing, without any other concern." He held out his hand.

"You helped send her away," I whispered. I looked away from him.

"Jasper?" Delphine asked.

"My wishes still stand. Regardless of what happens between Melasina and I, if you exile them again, I will be exiled as well."

"Why?" Delphine asked again.

"Because standing with them is the right thing to do, regardless of the outcome," Jasper looked at me, his eyes pleading.

"Your request has been noted," Delphine said. "We thank you for your honesty. But I must ask that you allow the Cormiers to leave, as we have much more to discuss."

Jasper held my eyes with his, seeking a sign, wanting something I couldn't give.

"Thank you," I said to Delphine. Then I took my mother's hand, turned away from Jasper Thibodeaux and walked out of the door. It closed behind me without another word from Jasper.

I did not look back.

CHAPTER TWELVE

Jasper

*W*atching Melasina and her mother and the talking skull walk away from me was the hardest thing that I'd ever done. I wanted to run after her, to beg for her forgiveness.

But that wasn't why I'd said what I said. I knew when I shared my part in her mother's exile that she might never want anything to do with me again.

I had to be honest. I had to stand up for me, for what I wanted, and what I knew was right.

And it looked like I had gambled, and lost.

Over the next week, I practically lived at Magnolia House. Two days after my confession in the meeting room, my magic righted itself. So I'd been right, facing my fears of rejection, of being nothing, of being cast out for doing the right thing. I did as Lavinia had instructed me weeks earlier, and I spent the day casting spells for everything. By the end of the day, I knew my magic was back, and the way it should be. I knew that I'd broken the curse.

It was too bad I might have broken my own heart in the process.

I sighed, and kept on with the meetings, and the discussions, and the questioning of Talia, and all the things that had to happen. As all this was going on, witches from the coven were asking to meet with Delphine and the elders to confess their fears.

We were healing, slowly.

After that first week, I went by the house on Saint Ann's. Sariah was walking out the front door. She saw me, and her face lit up in a smile.

At least one of the Cormiers was glad to see me.

"Is Mel here?" I asked.

"Yes, and she's got her magic back, so go in at your own peril," Sariah said. "I've explained to her that if it weren't for you, I wouldn't be here. But she's mad still."

"She's allowed to be," I said.

"Wise man," Sariah patted my arm. "Go on in. Just be ready for things to fly."

I nodded, and watched her walk down the street. She seemed so... normal. Which was not what I expected from a woman who'd been under a spell for fourteen years.

Guilt washed over me.

"It's nice to see her back home, isn't it?" Mel was at the door, her arms crossed.

"It is. It's why I went to get her," I said.

"You wouldn't have had to do that if you hadn't been part of sending her away," Mel said, her face expressionless.

"I know," I said. "May I please come in and talk to you?"

"No," she said. "You can say your piece right here."

"Out in public?" I asked.

"Take it or leave it," Mel's face was stone.

I sighed, and then straightened my shoulders. "All right. I'm sorry. I believed Talia. I was only seventeen when she worked on this case, and I had no reason to doubt her. She rescued me from my own hell," I said. "And I'll be happy to tell you all about it, in great detail, if you'd like. The point is, she rescued me. She gave me a life when I was looking at a pretty bleak one. I had a home, and food, and clothing, and a chance at being something." I tried to keep my voice steady. "She was like my mom," I finished. "If you think I enjoyed what I did, I didn't. I lost the only mom I've known for nearly fifteen years. She spits when she sees me now. I lost a chance with you. But I still did the right thing, because I knew it was about more than looking like I was doing the right thing, or making the right moves. I had to do the right thing. For you, for your mom, and even for me." My head dropped. I looked back up.

"So that's it. I'm sorry. I screwed up. I was more concerned with appearances than doing the right thing for years. I want to try again. I'm just asking for a chance." I looked into her eyes.

"Please."

Then I shut up. I wanted to go on, to keep telling her why giving me another shot was the best idea, but I didn't say a word.

This was Mel's decision. It couldn't be anything else.

Her lips twisted, and she looked away. "Fine. Come in," Mel said, and disappeared from the doorway.

A wide grin spread across my face as I raced up the small porch to the door. I had a chance.

That was all I needed.

EPILOGUE

Melasina
Six Months Later

I smiled, listening to my mom and Jasper talk. We'd had dinner out in the courtyard. It was dark, but the light strings overhead gave us enough light. There were also candles flickering on the table. My mom laughed at something Jasper said.

"Not bad," I murmured toward where Zelda's reliquary sat on its stand.

I'd gotten her a stand that fit the box, and we moved the stand around the house. She liked to be where we were, to be in the middle of what was going on. I counted her as a friend, one that meant a great deal. Along with my mom and Jasper.

I wished my dad could be here, but my parents were not able to mend their fences as Jasper and I had. I knew Mom was having lunch with him occasionally but other than that, I wasn't aware of their having much of a relationship. It made me sad, but I understood. There were some bridges that took longer to cross.

"Maybe he's not a magic stealer," Zelda said grudgingly.

While I'd forgiven Jasper, and given him a chance, Zelda held onto grudges longer than I did. She didn't trust him, even after my magic came back.

It had taken a few days after the meeting at Magnolia House for my ability to do any sort of magic to return. I'd been in bed and my alarm went off. I reached out, and I was too far away to hit the snooze button.

"Snooze," I said.

The alarm went off.

I sat up.

The next hour was spent casting magic all over the house. After an hour and at least fifty spells, I was pretty sure my magic was back.

Thank Goddess.

"I don't think that's what he stole," I said to Zelda.

I heard the wheezing sound that was her laugh.

Jasper turned to look at me. "What's so funny?"

"Girl talk, boy. Girl talk," Zelda said.

That made Mom and me laugh.

Jasper's face turned serious. "I'm glad we're all here," he said. "I wanted to talk with you, Mel."

"Why don't we go inside, Z?" Mom said, getting up and reaching for the reliquary stand.

Jasper held out a hand. "No, I'd really like you to stay."

Mom sat back into her seat slowly.

Jasper looked back to me, and leaned forward, taking my hands. "I'm so glad you gave me another chance, Mel. I would have understood if you hadn't—"

"Lucky doesn't cover it," Zelda muttered.

I waved at her.

"But I'm so glad you did. This past six months has been the best of my life. And I want that for the rest of my life."

The entire garden was silent, almost as though it was holding its breath.

Jasper slid down out of his chair onto one knee and pulled something sparkling from his pocked in one swift movement. "Will you marry me? I love you, I love everything about you. There is no one for me but you, and if you'll have me, I'm yours for the rest of your life." He held out the sparkly thing, which turned out to be a large solitaire diamond ring.

I could see that my had her hands clasped in front of her.

Leaning down, I held out my hand. "Yes," I said.

Jasper slid the ring on, pulling me to him and into his lap as he did.

"How do you move like that?" I whispered into his ear.

"How about I show you later?" he growled into mine, taking a nip of my earlobe.

I felt my body thrill at his touch, a touch that would be mine for the rest our lives.

∼

Dyan Chick
Wicked Creatures

I swore off relationships when I was thirteen. And now, as I wait for coffee in the world's worst bridesmaid dress, I meet the first man who's ever made me question my choice.
He's the physical manifestation of every male fantasy I've ever had. Which was why I bolted before the sparks could turn into flames. He was dangerous. I could sense it. Everything about him would not only destroy my commitment to be single forever, it would destroy everything else I'd been working for.
When a dark curse by a rogue witch forces us together, I know I'm screwed. I have to get away from him before the curse binds together us forever. Or worse, before I fall in love.

You've just read a bit of Dyan Chick's Wicked Creatures.
Pick it up today here:
WICKED CREATURES

The Coven thanks you for reading WICKED LOVE. You won't **believe** what we have coming next. Want a sneak peek? Check out our website at midnightcoven.com.

There are thirteen different books in the Cursed Coven series, each penned by one of today's hottest paranormal romance authors. While each story stands on its own with a happily ever after, characters do tend to wander from book to book, and you don't want to miss a cameo by one of your favorites.You can read the novellas in any order.

The Coven will return soon with a twisted collaboration that will keep you reading all night long. Until then, enjoy the snippet from WICKED CREATURES, found at the end of WICKED LOVE.

The magic continues with each witch who falls under our curse. Find your favorite now!

Wicked Thorne by K. Loraine
Wicked Warlock by Marina Simcoe
Wicked Love by Lisa Manifold
Wicked Creatures by Dyan Chick
Wicked Omens by Patricia D. Eddy
Wicked Devotion by Renea Mason
Wicked Desires by K.L. Bone
Wicked Hunt by Alice K. Wayne
Wicked Truth by Corinne O'Flynn
Wicked Witch by Jessie Lane
Wicked Shadows by Ariel Marie
Wicked Hexes by Amelia Hutchins
Wicked Charm by Knox & Miers

Do you want to keep up to date with all of our releases? Join our Facebook Group. We'd love to see you there!

ABOUT THE AUTHOR

Lisa Manifold is a *USA Today* Bestselling Author of fantasy, paranormal, and romance stories. She moved to Colorado as an adult and has no plans of living anywhere else. She is a consummate reader, often running late because "Just one more page!" She is a fan of all things Con, and has an entire room devoted to the costumes created for Cons.

Lisa is the author of many flavors of paranormal series, including The Realm, Djinn Everlasting, Dragon Thief, The Aumahnee Prophecy, Tales from the Veil, Sisters of the Curse, the books from The Midnight Coven collective, the Deadwood Sisters and The Mostly Open Paranormal Investigative Agency.

She lives as close to the mountains as possible with her husband, children, and four red rescue dogs.

Stay in touch:
Sign up for my Newsletter and never miss a thing!
Website: www.lisamanifold.com
Or one of the links below.
Xoxo
Lisa

ALSO BY LISA MANIFOLD

The Midnight Coven Stories

(books written with a collective of authors)

Cursed Coven Series

Wicked Love

Vampire Mates Series

Immortal Darkness

Vampire Brides Series

Forever Blood

The Mostly Open Paranormal

Investigative Agency

Dark Pact

Dark Night (Nov 2019)

Deadwood Sisters

Hellborn: The Unlucky Book 1

Hellfire: The Unlucky Book 2

Hellfury: The Unlucky Book 3 (Dec 2019)

Dragon Thief

Dragon Lost

Dragon Found

Hidden Wishes

Sisters of the Curse

Thea's Tale

One Night at the Ball

Casimir's Journey

Do you like being in the loop? Sign up for Lisa's newsletter! Shenanigans, book recs, and the latest news abound!

Want to see more of Lisa's books?

Visit www.Lisamanifold.com